MYTHS TO LIE BY

Short Pieces

DOROTHY BRYANT

ATA BOOKS

Ata Books
1928 Stuart Street
Berkeley, California 94703

Cover Photo: Filicia Liu
Cover Design: Robert Bryant
Editorial and Production: Betty Bacon
Anne Fox
Lorri Ungaretti
Kathy Vergeer
Typesetting: Ann Flanagan Typography

Contents

Foreword

This collection includes five essays, seven reviews, seven stories, a play, and a letter. Thirteen of the twenty-one pieces have been published elsewhere, but, since these are often the shorter ones, over half the contents of this book appears in print for the first time. I wrote most of these pieces between 1973 and 1983, but three were written during the 1960s.

The title *Myths to Lie By* comes from the first essay and is a respectful takeoff on the title of a book by Joseph Campbell, *Myths to Live By.* I chose that title because so many of the pieces touch the theme of myth making and unmaking.

"Myth" is a shifty word. Among its many definitions, there are two opposing ones. Myth can mean the symbolic expression of a deep reality. A true myth. This is the sense in which Joseph Campbell uses the word. It can also mean a commonly held but mistaken belief. A false myth. Thomas Szasz used the word this way in the title *The Myth of Mental Illness.*

The word can even be used in both ways at the same time. Take, for instance, the biblical myth of Adam and Eve. No doubt the myth expresses deep realities of human development: that the emergence from animal unconsciousness coincides with sexual awakening; that intellectual curiosity and agonizing childbirth are related, one the prize, the other the penalty for upright stature, and so on. A true myth. But these realities are stated in the form of a story used to justify a long history of oppression. A false myth. Hence a myth which symbolizes profound truths promulgates a pernicious lie.

Perhaps the very use of language leads us into lying, since even the best verbal statements are mere approximations of parts of the truth glimpsed momentarily. Sometimes it seems that the verbal statements which come closest to truth are those which locate and correct the errors of earlier verbal statements. At any rate, that description fits much of the writing in this book: the challenging of what I see as commonly held, unexamined, dubious ideas. Unmaking false myths. I hope that once or twice during that process I manage to recreate or rediscover an expression of reality—a true myth.

FALSE MYTHS
and
TRUE HEROES

Myths to Lie By

In 1980 I published a novel called *Prisoners* about a relationship woven through correspondence between a convict and a middle-aged liberal, a relationship that quickly unravels when the convict is paroled. Last July, publication of *In the Belly of the Beast,* letters from convict Jack Abbott to Norman Mailer, occurred almost simultaneously with the fatal stabbing of a young playwright by the just-released Abbott.

Now I am often asked, in light of strong parallels between *Prisoners* and the Abbott case, to comment on this real-life tragedy. I leave comments on prison reform and convict reentry to those people who work and live with the daily problems of these movements as professionals, volunteers, relatives of convicts and convicts themselves. I am not one of them. As a literary person, I would like to limit myself to discussing certain myths held and expressed by some literary people, myths that may express a psychological truth but which, misapplied, often obscure our understanding of facts in the real world.

One of these I call the Myth of the Outlaw Hero. The Outlaw Hero is at war with oppressive institutions, often with all institutions. He is McMurphy in *One Flew Over the Cuckoo's Nest,* refusing to conform to standards of "sanity" laid down by castrating Nurse Ratched of the mental ward. Or he is *Cool Hand Luke,* with the appeal of Paul Newman, refusing to be humiliated by gross, sadistic prison guards. Or Bonnie and Clyde, whose bank robberies become symbolic attacks on capitalists. We can trace this tradition back through *The Petrified Forest,* the movie in which Bogart created the modern gangster hero, admired, rationalized, mythologized by the intellectual Leslie Howard, who identified with him. The tradition goes further back through various cowboy shootists, real and imagined, and ultimately, I suppose, back to Robin Hood.

All Outlaw Heroes have two traits in common. The first is that they never compromise. Unlike the rest of us, who alternate between asserting ourselves and submitting, as survival demands (more than survival demands, to our shame), the Outlaw Hero always asserts himself, defies authority, defends his honor, his manhood, ready to "die on his feet rather than live on his knees." And that brings me to the second trait: all Outlaw Heroes get killed, except Robin Hood, who did bow to his rightful king when the usurper was deposed. We never learn whether Robin Hood had trouble adjusting to law-abiding life after all those years in Sherwood Forest. We don't want to know, just as we prefer our Outlaw Heroes safely dead after they have enacted our inner craving for uncompromising, heroic, unbending defiance.

But it is one thing to construct mythical heroes to act out our urges and relieve our frustrations at the complexity of our lives. It is another thing to confuse these one-dimensional symbolic inventions with real human beings, projecting our longings for freedom on people who are no more free than we are. The danger is that we may mistake symptoms of pathology (rigidity, aggression, destructive compulsions) for signs of being "...the proudest, bravest, most daring, most enterprising and the most undefeated of the poor," as Norman Mailer refers to Abbott in his introduction to the book.

Another myth, which may be of nineteenth century origin, is what I call the Oliver Twist Myth. You remember Dickens's little Oliver, half-starved in an orphanage, kidnapped by Fagin and trained to be a thief, is finally rescued, bathed, fed and given a home where he will live happily ever after. Dickens's purpose was clear and laudable—to show the awful conditions for children of the poor. The myth, the mistaken assumption, is that the rescued Oliver could fit right into middle-class English society, that no residual anger or bad habits picked up from the gang would mar his adjustment.

Under the influence of the Oliver Twist Myth, we not only (rightly) condemn the institutions that injure the child, we assume that all we need do is release the victim. So that Mailer could read Jack Abbott's description of himself as a hardened "state-raised" killer, and conclude that, "It is certainly time for him to get out."

Another myth allied to the Oliver Twist Myth I would call the Myth of the Class-War Outlaw. We know that our prisons are full of poor criminals, not rich ones. The military mass murderers go free and decorated, the tycoon takes his millions from us in perfect freedom. Granted. But it is a mistake to reason from this fact that because only poor people are in prison, prisoners are representative of the poor. In fact, only a very small proportion of the poor are in prison, and they differ from the vast majority of the poor in that they broke some law. And—this is very important—they rarely broke the law as Robin Hood did, stealing from the rich to give to the poor. They stole from the poor, they assaulted the poor, they killed the poor.

Mailer poses the penitentiary against the "prisons" where "the middle class retires into walled cities with armed guards." In the Myth of the Class-War Outlaw we romanticize him as the enemy of our enemy—the smug, philistine, reactionary American. The reality is quite different. Jack Abbott did not approach any walled cities, or even any unwalled middle-income apartment house. He killed a man who was working in a restaurant on Manhattan's Lower East Side.

The last myth I must take up may be the most dangerous of all. It is the Myth of the Power of the Word. I do not mean the power the word has over the world. When I write of the Power of the Word, I mean its power to redeem or even to exalt the proficient user of the word. If you read Jack Abbott's letters, you will find on every page his assertion that he is capable of, perhaps compelled toward, acts of violence exactly like the one he committed a few weeks after his release. Yet the literary people who widely reviewed and lauded this book were shocked when the tragedy came. What magic did they think had been wrought by the Power of the Word?

Do we writers believe that the ability to manipulate words confers moral superiority? Perhaps we believe that the use of words has some purging, purifying quality—that by expressing certain feelings eloquently we purge ourselves of them, emerging free, as if newly born and innocent. Or is it that our writers—too many of them—have written so many elegant fictions of sadism, cruelty, pornography, violence and death while sitting in quiet little rooms, that we think words don't mean anything—that writers aren't supposed to mean what they write?

Worst of all, have we so romanticized the writer that mere facility with words—no matter what awful truths or seductive lies they tell—confers the status of a mythic hero, superior to the less verbally articulate masses of human beings? If so, with this final myth we writers have lost our function as the voice for those masses, cutting through their evasions and fears and lies to uncover the truth at the heart of humanity.

* * *

"Myths to Lie By" was written at the request of Peter Carroll, then book editor of the *San Francisco Bay Guardian,* which printed it in 1981.

* * *

My review of Malcolm Braly's autobiography, published five years earlier in the *San Francisco Review of Books,* touches another side of the "prisoner" theme. I had finished my novel *Prisoners* a year before Braly's book came out. I felt encouraged by the support his first-hand account gave to my fictional one. And I was excited by discovering a strong writer whose work I had so far missed.

Writing book reviews is usually an unrewarding chore. The reviewer is poorly paid, cramped by space limitations, and rushed by a deadline which must conform to publication date of the book. In the following review and in the six others included in this book, I was nevertheless able to "take the occasion of reviewing to reflect on the intellectual and moral issues that beset us" (as Denis Donoghue so gracefully put it in a recent *New York Times Book Review*). The chance for such reflection makes writing the review interesting and makes reprinting it worthwhile.

Malcolm Braly's *False Starts:*
A Memoir of San Quentin and Other Prisons

"I was, from any beginning I can recall, a liar, a sneak, a show-off and a thief."

Malcolm Braly was first arrested at sixteen when his stolen coat was recognized in a poolhall he frequented. He told the owner and the police that he had bought the coat from a transient, then went home to bed, knowing the police would come and discover his loot from other burglaries. He drew two years at Preston (which he entered with a book of poetry under his arm), escaped once, was picked up in a cul-de-sac behind a store he planned to rob, and was returned to Preston (a boys' reform school which sounds like the cruelest of the prisons he has seen).

Freed at nineteen in 1944, he easily found work and boosted his income with burglaries. Finally, he joined two Preston alumni for a Keystone Cops armed robbery run from Sacramento, California, to Austin, Nevada. Locking the sheriff in his own jail, Braly boasted, "We'll be back." And he was—arrested within a few hours and lucky to be still alive. He did time first in Nevada, then back in California on essentially the same charge. During this term he started painting and writing.

Paroled from San Quentin at twenty-six, he went to San Francisco, where he married, fathered a son, worked as a sign painter, and burglarized stores. He was arrested in an all-night diner where he and his partner sat after a suburban burglary (while every instinct warned him to get out of an area where he was so conspicuous). He was thirty-one the next time he got out. He took up with a sixteen-year-old girl who loved dressing up in the fancy clothes his stolen money bought and who cried for him when he was arrested for a burglary of medical offices. This time the police were led to him by a slip of paper he had dropped at the burglary scene; on the slip of paper were his name and address! During the term he finished a book, sold it, and was transferred to a minimum security conservation camp.

At thirty-seven he was paroled, solvent, reunited with his sister (the only family he'd known since age fourteen), and he had good prospects for a future as a writer. A year later he was back in prison for a series of minor parole violations.

Now it seemed clear to me I had always known I was going to jail...When I had told Percy (the sheriff), "We'll be back," I had known. When I had followed George into the all-night diner, I had known...I proved it again when I dropped my address on the floor of the doctor's office and went home to wait for the police. Finally, I had cheerfully provided the Parole Officer with the rope he needed to hang me.

I had served more time for a handful of inept burglaries than most men would have served for killing a police officer, and the prison, which I had hated so deeply and scored so bitterly for its every failing, was only my chosen instrument in the willful destruction of my own life.

By now it is clear that the "Other Prisons" of the subtitle include metaphorical prisons more incorrigibly destructive than most in our penal system. Yet even after this clear insight into the prisons of his mind, discharged at age forty, with his writing career still intact and promising, Braly had not quite won his freedom. He watched himself withdrawing, lying in bed, going broke, drifting downward again. Botching a burglary, he barely escaped being caught by police.

...I landed in a small stand of underbrush, and crawled deeper into this thin cover to lie gasping with exhaustion...How grotesque I seemed to myself. The boy who had climbed the sides of buildings with such a reckless heart was gone, and in his place had appeared this middle-aged man who knew only one way to fail.

This time he rescued himself, wiring his agent for money to flee across the continent to New York. The reader supposes this putting of distance between himself and the scene of his crimes was importantly symbolic. Braly does not say. His story, except for a brief coda, ends here. Now, eight years later, with five books published, a wife and family, and a modest fame which includes appearances on TV shows, "The pattern is clearly broken."

If we assume that Braly represents a certain minority of fuck-ups our society produces, we can find many reasons for this talented man's thirty years on the brink of suicide: a chaotic, abandoned childhood; a prison system that teaches only dependence upon it; an outside world with no support for ex-convicts; an illogical, politics-ridden parole system; and society's general corruption, vindictiveness and plain stupidity. All true and applicable. But what pops into my mind simultaneously is Leonard Woolf's observation on Virginia Woolf's attacks of suicidal madness: "...practically all Virginia's insane symptoms were exaggerations of psychological phenomena observable in a large number of people."

14

I am struck, not by Braly's difference from those of us who have never been locked up, but by his similarity to the rest of us. (I speak, of course, of that minority of the earth's human population who have choices beyond bare survival.) As I approach his age, I count the varieties of self-destruction indulged in by failure addicts. The more obvious may actually be addicted to some deadening narcotic like alcohol or power or self-help books. More subtle are those who embark on projects (a marriage, a book, a change) and then cunningly build the barrier which will defeat them inches from their goal. Hardest to spot are those who apparently achieve "success" while, to use an old-fashioned expression, losing their own souls. Most of us have been in those "Other Prisons" Braly hints at. The difference between him and us lies in the subtlety with which we build them, lock ourselves in, and deny their existence as part of the act of throwing away the key.

Are any immune? We all seem to some degree overtaken at about puberty by a life-and-death struggle. Some of us, like Braly, emerge from the battle relatively whole and aimed toward life, toward ourselves, at about forty. But the grim fact is that most do not. And none of the current psychological or social explanations of failure explains this mass suicide.

On bad days I lean toward an evolutionary theory, a kind of psychological Darwinism: so many billion attempts at creating a human being, most doomed to failure. But there is something inhuman in accepting such vast and ruthless waste. I can't believe that any human being is necessarily sentenced to life imprisonment in his or her chosen pattern of failure.

Perhaps the real question this book poses is not how did Braly get onto his self-destructive merry-go-round, but how did he, unlike the majority of people, get off? He had help, which he finally learned to use. He had luck in possessing a talent that made possible a career outside the mundane job world he could not stand. And he aged. In his description of his final burglary attempt, he gives the impression that the fears and cravings that drove him had been blunted by middle age. Above all, somehow, a decision was made when he fled east. But none of these answers suffices. And I find myself applauding Braly's refusal to offer any easy solution to this mystery.

I can't answer my own question. At the end of his long life, Jung wrote that the individual was the only reality. If I sense this truth precisely, it says my life, as all lives are, is unique. For myself, I would change nothing because it has all led me to become the man I hoped to be.

The next review is one of my early myth-busting efforts. It was printed in *Freedom News* in late 1968.

Freedom News, circulation three thousand monthly, came out of the basement of Betty and Mayer Segal of Kensington, California. It was one of the many "underground" papers that sprang up in the sixties in reaction to the managed or absent news of the major media, a blackout of facts far worse than anything we experience today.

It was in *Freedom News* that I first saw my words in print. In 1968 the Segals asked me to review a play at the old Berkeley Repertory Theatre. Ashamed to admit I didn't know how, I somehow wrote the review. For the next five years I reviewed books, films, plays—often in odd combinations of my choice, with no regard to publication date and no limits on length. Everything I contributed was printed, and no one changed a word without consulting me. The Segals's editorial policy coupled high standards for writing with high respect for even the least experienced effort.

What *Freedom News* did for me is far greater than anything I did for it. So I print "The New Cliches" with respectful gratitude and with consciousness of my good luck at writing under ideal conditions, never duplicated since.

The review itself was heresy to the liberals (that is, my friends) who read *Freedom News.* It not only attacked three cherished films, but more strongly attacked audience reaction to them. Two of these films still show up occasionally on TV. I don't know what the audience response to them is now.

The New Cliches

In a recent interview Tom Luddy of the [Berkeley] Telegraph Repertory Cinema said he showed many old movies because "I prefer the old cliches to the new ones." I don't know that I prefer the old ones over the new ones, but the old cliches had at least one thing going for them: no one took them seriously. The new cliches are taken seriously, and that's why it's time we examined them carefully. Typical of the new cliches are three films, spread over the last two years, but still shown and discussed widely and taken seriously by people who favor radical political and social change (or who say they do): *The Graduate, If,* and *Easy Rider.*

The heroes of these films are young; they are threatened and oppressed by the old and by The System (the two often being inseparable). *The Graduate* is bugged by his parents, the students in *If* by teachers and older students, the Easy Riders by rednecks and police. The heroes are also male. The women in these films are sexually aggressive bitches (Anne Bancroft in *The Graduate*) or compliant sex partners (the waitress in *If* and the commune girls and whores in *Easy Rider*). Except for the silly mother in *The Graduate,* they are solely sex objects.

As in many male fantasies, wheels are important. In *The Graduate* we have the sportscar ride up the California coast to Berkeley. In *If* the ride is shorter, but takes place on a stolen motorcycle, an important transition, for in *Easy Rider,* of course, the motorcycle becomes the central character, the symbol of free manhood. (I remember a Hells Angel once innocently saying of his bike how he felt great "with all that power between my legs.") All three rides are idyllic, wind-blown travelogues through some miraculous country which is (as another reviewer pointed out) devoid of billboard signs, beer cans, fences, or industrial sprawl. In the English setting of *If* the motorcycle cuts across beautifully manicured park areas—the audience never sees the wake of ripped up lawns it must leave behind.

But with all of this, and admitting that I am a female who hates the very sound of a motorcycle, I am ready to identify with these heroes in their battle against the system or whatever threatens them. But I cannot.

Because I do not like them.

I do not like the at least twenty-two-year-old graduate who despises his parents while refusing to do anything but float in their swimming pool or in their neighbor's bed, while claiming the innocence of a fourteen-year-old virgin seduced by the Wicked Witch of the West. I do not like the students (*If*) who plaster the walls of their rooms with Vietnam atrocity pictures and then sit drinking vodka, never lifting a finger to help younger students right next door who are being terrorized. I am only impressed by their strong stomachs. I do not like drug pushers (the stuff in *Easy Rider* had to be heroin or cocaine). And I am unimpressed by two bikers with a gas tank full of money who freeload at the commune where it appears food will soon be in short supply, and look down their noses at everyone while never lifting a finger or a dollar bill to help anyone.

In fact I have always found it impossible to identify with people who moralistically judge others while they themselves are guilty of cruelty, insensitivity, and exploitation of others. In old movies (and in many books) such characters were cast as hypocritical, fundamentalist clergymen or frozen maiden aunts and were usually comic figures; occasionally they were taken seriously (as in Maugham's *Rain*) but they were never treated sympathetically, let alone turned into heroes.

Indeed the creators of these films seem to have doubts about their heroes. Mike Nichols was quoted in *The New Yorker* as saying that his Graduate would end up exactly like his parents. (Why do young audiences cheer when he rides off with the girl next door—which is exactly what his parents had been trying to force him to do?) The key line of *Easy Rider* is Peter Fonda's "We blew it." But the comment is never pursued, and when I discussed the film with a group of young college students, they admitted that they not only had never questioned that line, they had forgotten it! In *If* the ambivalence of the filmmakers is even more obvious, there being no clear line between the acts of the students and their fantasies. Serious discussion of the values of the heroes is therefore impossible. ("Oh, but they didn't really do that; it was one of their fantasies.")

I have already mentioned the confusing ending of *The Graduate*. The other two films have similarly strange endings. In *If*, the three vodka drinkers finally are moved to action after taking a beating from the older students who enforce the discipline of the school. Their action? They find a convenient cache of ammunition and proceed to bomb and machine-gun teachers, parents, and students. (But this may be only a fantasy? Yeah, forget it.)

If the ending of *If* is hard to deal with, the ending of *Easy Rider* is impossible. After saying "We blew it," the two bikers are back on the road, where they are overtaken by two rednecks and shot. Peter Fonda goes out in a burst of flame; his friend dies more messily.

What does this mean? Don't go into the South with long hair? America is violent? Both statements may be true, but they do not fit this film. The sudden victimization of the riders makes no sense.

I do not mean to say that such things do not happen in real life. They do. But in the fictional context of this film, such an ending does nothing except to shock the audience into suspension of critical faculties.

And that is exactly what it was intended to do. By obliterating the central characters, the film tries to wipe out questions which it had begun to raise about these characters. The important question to ask yourself when you see this film is, "How would I feel toward these two guys if they were not killed?" That question raises more important and uncomfortable questions which, if the filmmakers tried to deal with them, might seriously diminish the popularity of this film with young people.

Popularity is, of course, the key to the basic dishonesty of all three films. They are meant to be commercial successes, and in the tradition of the movies they make romantic heroes act out the fantasies of the audience they hope to attract. This audience seems to be made up of people, mostly young but some old, who like to think of themselves as rebels, but who will take their rebellion quietly, thank you, at the movies, cheering the machine-gunners.

Like the drunken lawyer in *Easy Rider,* they see long hair and the wandering motorcycle and contempt for their elders as symbols of freedom, but they prefer the symbol to the act. Symbols are easy. Freedom is hard. Acts are difficult, complicated, requiring thought and responsibility, and little of the exhilaration of a simple battle between good guys and bad guys, young and old, long hair and short.

I began this article by saying that these films were worth discussing because so many good people were taking them seriously. Hemingway once said that the major requirement of a writer was that he be "unbullshitable." I would like to suggest a reevaluation of these films, based on the assumption that the same requirement is necessary for any people, young or old, who want to see a real change for the better in the quality of our lives.

* * *

19

Along with being an interesting and well written book, *Farewell to Manzanar* did something important for me. It gave me a chance to write about the deep shame which I, and all other Californians born before World War II, have carried ever since, whether silent or spoken, conscious or unconscious, within victim or persecutor or silent bystander. My review of this book appeared in *The Nation* in 1974.

Jeanne and James Houston's
Farewell to Manzanar

I have forgotten the names of nearly all my seventh-grade classmates, except that of Yoshio, who disappeared suddenly one day in 1942. My parents and teachers explained all the sinister differences that made it necessary to remove Japanese-Americans (but not Italian-Americans like us) from the West Coast, for the sake of my safety. But I knew they were lying, even if they did not seem to know it.

In the late 1950s, teaching in a San Francisco high school, I mentioned the Japanese-American internment. My students gaped, then laughed. I had invented it. It had never, could never, happen here. Suddenly I realized the extent of the blackout of this shameful episode. "It never happened" meant that the deep, unexamined shame I had felt ever since the disappearance of Yoshio was felt by all Californians of my generation. I assigned the homework: "Go home and ask your parents."

My students (male, average I.Q. 120 and all Caucasian but two Chinese) returned the next day, informed but defiant, and said, yes, it happened, *but*. Then they repeated all the racist rationalizations I remembered from 1942, word for word. "But you don't believe that nonsense!" I exclaimed. Their eyes shifted away from mine, and their faces closed. The lies, the defense, the justifications, and the underlying shame seemed to have been passed on to the next generation.

The silence regarding this disgrace seemed imposed by Japanese-Americans as well. Books on the subject were few and never sold well. It was as though the victims themselves felt ashamed of their persecution, never mentioned it, and seldom read or wrote about it. Perhaps that same undefined, unexamined shame kept me from reading much on the subject until I picked up *Farewell to Manzanar.*

Jeanne Wakatsuki was seven years old when her family was taken from their Long Beach home to a desert encampment called Manzanar, where they lived for three and a half years. Jeanne adjusted without quite knowing there was anything to adjust to. "At seven I was too young to be insulted." The experiences she recalls now, thirty years later, must be among the hardest for anyone to come to terms with: the deep hurt without cruel intent, almost without awareness of injury, more deeply damaging because of this very lack of awareness.

For example, internees were not starved like their European counterparts, but the abundant mess-hall eating was nevertheless deeply destructive. "...We would eat in gangs with the other kids, while the grownups sat at another table. I confess I enjoyed this part of it at the time. We all did. A couple of years after the camps opened, sociologists studying the life noticed what had happened to the families...edicts went out that families must start eating together again....It was too late....My own family, after three years of mess-hall living, collapsed as an integrated unit."

Life at Manzanar was full of the contradictions that may be ultimately harder to cope with than outright brutality. There was the very American school yearbook, with a barbed-wire design on the cover. There were dancing classes and criminally inadequate medical facilities. There were, eventually, lush gardens and orchards, where men like Jeanne's father squatted in alcoholic despair. In 1942 the internees had arrived paralyzed by shock and fear. In 1945 many had to be forced to leave, paralyzed by fear of life outside. A matching irony permeates the bits of family history woven into the story, from the arrival of Jeanne's father in America in 1905 to the visit of Jeanne's brother to the ancestral hometown in 1946, "the ash heap of Hiroshima."

It was not until years after leaving the camp, back in Long Beach, in her last year of high school, that Jeanne had her first glimpse of the shadowy paradoxes she would have to sort out in order to find herself. Both by using racial stereotypes and fighting them, she managed to be elected carnival queen. At her moment of triumph—the procession over bed sheets, toward the plywood throne in the high school gym—she was almost overwhelmed by cold clarity:

> I stepped out into blue light.... The gym was packed and
> the lights were intense. Suddenly it was too hot out there....
> The throne seemed blocks away, and now the dress was stifling
> me.... What was I doing out there anyway.... I wanted to
> laugh. I wanted to cry. I wanted to be ten years old again, so
> I could believe in princesses and queens.... I wanted the carn-
> ival to end.... But all eyes were on me. It was too late now not
> to follow this make-believe carpet to its plywood finale, and I
> did not yet know of any truer destination.

James Houstin, Jeanne's husband and co-author, is quoted in the foreword: "The issue isn't what we wanted to write about," but rather the private human experience. *Farewell to Manzanar* succeeds with such grace in this effort because the Houstons were not simply trying to communicate facts as Jeanne knew them, but were themselves on a search to touch the truth of her experience, to examine it, and to understand it wholly. The great strength of the book is the sense it gives the reader of being allowed to accompany Jeanne on this most personal and intimate journey.

Jeanne tells this striking anecdote about her mother. The family had been given forty-eight hours to leave their home, and the predators were closing in. A second-hand dealer "prowling around for weeks, like...(a wolf)," offered her fifteen dollars for a "fine old set of china, blue and white porcelain, almost translucent." There was no possibility of taking it along.

> He said fifteen was his top price...she just glared at this
> man, all the rage and frustration channeled at him through her
> eyes.... She reached into the red velvet case, took out a dinner
> plate and hurled it at the floor right in front of his feet.
> The man leaped back shouting, "Hey! Hey, don't do that!
> Those are valuable dishes!"
> Mama took out another dinner plate and hurled it at the
> floor, then another and another, just quivering and glaring at
> the retreating dealer, with tears streaming down her cheeks.
> He finally turned and scuttled out the door, heading for the
> next house. When he was gone she stood there smashing cups
> and bowls and platters until the whole set lay in scattered
> blue and white fragments across the wooden floor.

* * *

The genesis of the next essay will interest readers who are curious about how writing projects get started, then wander from the original intent, often feeding into other projects.

In 1979 I had (yet again!) begun the autobiographical novel I thought I ought to have done already. An admirer of Samuel Butler, I followed his example of a leisurely opening covering what I knew about my ancestors. I got as far as my birth when I was stopped cold by the doctor who delivered me, Doctor Nellie Null, a woman I hadn't thought of for years. Suddenly I was full of curiosity about her, and I began the search for information that is described in the article itself.

My original intention was to do a biography of Doctor Nellie, perhaps in oral history. I set off with ignorant optimism and a tape recorder. At the time I was without a car, taking buses around San Francisco. That didn't bother me. On public transportation I can read or dream or spy on people for stories. What did bother me was running around and talking to so many people; I had grown used to working in long silences. Another problem was that many contacts had moved out of San Francisco. I would have to spend my weekends, when I had a car available, driving long distances.

I quickly learned that taking oral history is not as easy as it seems. People are nervous about a tape recorder. I needed to put tremendous time and energy into preparing them, relaxing them. Sometimes I sat for two hours while a person mumbled dull details I knew I couldn't use. Then, as I packed up to go, he or she would say, "Oh, one little thing I almost forgot is. . ." and we were finally ready to start. Oral historians need transcribers, and I couldn't afford one. I trailed home from these exhausting interviews and sat down to the typewriter for another long, hard transcribing session.

A more serious disadvantage should have been obvious from the beginning. Doctor Nellie died in 1964 at the age of ninety; there were no survivors to talk about her early years. Even the few who remembered her before the age of fifty had been very young at the time. Soon I developed another problem. Relatives who had begun by being cooperative were backing off, refusing me pictures and records. Perhaps they did not want to discuss the inevitable family conflicts which had arisen around this strong woman. I didn't blame them. I was not sure I wanted to either.

The project came to a dead halt. I had neither oral history nor material for a biography. I decided to forget the whole thing.

But I couldn't. I had met some wonderful people who were eager to tell stories about Doctor Nellie and about the old days in Bayview-Hunters Point, a part of San Francisco *never* covered in the guide books. I decided to take the material I had gathered and make a gift of it to these people, a gift in the form of an article in which I would name as many of my oral contributors as possible; it would be fun for them to see their names in print.

California Living printed the article in September 1979. The money they paid me just about covered my phone bill, gas, and bus fares. I had spent countless hours phoning, traveling, recording, transcribing, talking, writing. The result was a short article which was likely to be ignored by all but that segment of older San Franciscans who lived or had once lived in the least fashionable area of the City.

In 1983—four years later—I began a (not autobiographical) novel, began it over and over again, discarding all my starts because they felt wrong. Then suddenly I seemed to hear again the voices of Manuel Piver and Eloise Fontaine and all the others describing the old Hunters Point, and I knew I had the setting for the beginning of the novel I am working on now.

In Search of Doctor Nellie

It started while I was working on a story about my childhood. Suddenly an image flashed upon me: an old woman standing over my hospital bed where, full of self-pity as I woke to the pain of my tonsillectomy, I whispered an answer to her question.

"Speak up, girl! You can talk. Who am I?"

Shocked out of my self-pity, I did speak up. "Doctor Nellie Null."

She laughed, grunted, patted my arm and disappeared.

Who was Dr. Nellie Null? I began to question my mother about her. I located her son, a retired physician who supplied dates and names. I sent a letter to the *Examiner* and other papers asking, in effect, who remembers Doctor Nellie? The answers came from all over Northern California and beyond.

She was born Nellie Belle Hollenbeak, near Pittville, California in 1874, ten years after her parents had crossed the country in a covered wagon, their first two children dying on the way. Nellie and six more brothers and sisters grew up on a farm near Fall River Mills. Life on the farm, of course, meant hard work, broken up by school, by horse and wagon trips to Redding for supplies, and by recreation which more leisured city people might envy. Audry Munro, related to Nellie by marriage, remembers, "My Uncle Doug always talked about what a wonderful skater Nellie was. In the winter when Upper Lake near the Bucher Ranch froze, they had skating parties at night. They built bonfires along the way and skated up to Fort Bidwell and down to Lake City, about sixteen miles."

At eighteen Nellie married a young teacher, John G. Null, whose family owned a nearby farm. A few months later Nellie was certified to teach primary grades in Modoc County. She and John rode on horseback in winter to schools like the one-room schoolhouse at Goos Creek, and in the summer they furthered their own studies. Before long, Nellie had earned her California teaching credential. But what she really wanted, had always wanted, was to be a doctor. She saved money, borrowed some from her father, and urged new plans on her husband. In 1902 they went to San Francisco, moved into the Mission District, and enrolled in the College of Physicians and Surgeons. Nellie must have been virtually the only woman enrolled at the time. If she encountered problems because of her sex, she never, so far as I have learned, ever mentioned them to anyone.

Doctors Nellie and J. G. (as they came to be called by their patients) were ready for certification when the 1906 earthquake hit the City. From the Sixteenth Street hill they could see flames sprouting from the windows of the Fairmont Hotel, and they watched the fire spread toward them, stopping just short of where they lived. Their first patients were earthquake victims, many of them treated in tents set up in the Bayview-Hunters Point District, then called Butchertown.

Probably this experience led them to begin general practice there. Being country people, they might have been drawn to its rural atmosphere, its open land, its grassy slopes rolling down to the Bay, its mixture of truck farms and livestock, packing and shipping. Within a few years they had built their headquarters at 4346 Third Street (then called Railroad Avenue) on a triangular lot bounded by Kirkwood and Newhall. Their three-story flat-iron building had stores on the street level, medical offices on the second floor, and roomy living quarters for them on the third.

At that point in her mid-thirties, Nellie must have decided that if she wanted to have a family, time was running out. In 1910 her son John was born, followed by Gilbert in 1912, while the young doctors established their practice.

Who were their patients? Eloise Fontaine Hugentobler came to Butchertown from France in 1909. "My father worked in a tannery and my mother kept a boarding house. Later we got a house on Waterville Street at the bottom of a hill where the cattle were penned. They'd bring them in from the country and fatten them up on that hill. The rains would wash down some of that soil, and you should have seen the vegetables my father grew in that backyard!"

There were Swedes, too, fishermen who went to Alaska for months at a time, leaving their families to run up a bill at grocery stores like the one owned by Freida Cahill's mother. "When they came back, they paid the bills and celebrated, had good, happy times. Then next season, they'd go again." There were Germans, Swiss, Italians, who, according to another old resident, "planted vegetables everywhere. They didn't own the land, everything was open, everything south of Williams Street was vegetables." There were Maltese and Russians and Portuguese. People kept goats, hogs, chickens. They went duck hunting at Hunters Point, where Chinese shrimp fishermen gave away the smaller bits from their catch. "Nobody ever *bought* fish."

Jim Arvenites, who still lives in the house his immigrant Greek father built, remembers how all his classmates spoke different languages, unable to understand their teachers or each other. "For a long time I didn't know there was no school on Saturdays. I used to go down there, see nobody, wait around the schoolyard for a while, then go back home. I'd bring home report cards, vaccination forms; my folks couldn't read them, they just signed."

More patients came from the nearby Mission District and Visitacion Valley. Except for the Irish, few spoke English, and Doctor Nellie spoke only English. "No, she didn't understand their language, but she understood people. They all went to her." Or she to them, with a horse and buggy, at all hours of the day or night.

But if Dr. Nellie had found her element, her husband had not. In 1916 they were divorced. He left the area and remarried, but they never lost contact. In later years he turned to Nellie when he needed help, and, according to her son, Dr. John Null, every year she took her sons out to dinner for a cheerful celebration of her wedding anniversary. No irony or bitterness? Dr. John shakes his head. "My mother had no time for bitterness."

26

What was it like for John and Gilbert, growing up in Butcher-town? Manuel Piver was one of their playmates, and he describes playing baseball and a complicated game called Peewee in the empty lot across the street from Dr. Nellie's building. "Both corners were empty, the whole length of the block, about 200 yards deep. Sometimes we played hockey on the street. There were hardly any cars then. Kids would come up from Visitacion Valley on roller skates. I hardly saw Dr. Nellie, she was always on the go. I'd just see her stick her head out the window and call, 'John, Gilbert, time for dinner,' and they'd run in. Sometimes we'd walk over to Hunters Point and swim. There was good sandy beach, clean water. Worn-out ferry boats were run up on the beach. We'd strip them and build ourselves little cabins right on the beach."

A pleasant place, another former resident told me, "except on Mondays. They'd kill on Mondays, and there'd be that stench." (In the thirties, when I was growing up in the Mission, a shift of the wind would waft that slaughterhouse smell over the Mission, and my parents would say, "Smell Butchertown? That means rain.")

Norma Bacci Hemovich remembers that John and Gilbert often went along with Dr. Nellie when she made her rounds, and when Norma went to her office, ". . . we used to play with her boys while waiting for her to treat us."

Freida Cahill was one of the women Dr. Nellie hired to look after John and Gilbert when she could not take them along. "Dr. Nellie came into my mother's store and found me making candy for my nieces in the back. 'You're just the one I want,' she said. I was eighteen." Like many women after her, Freida lived off and on for years with Dr. Nellie, caring for the boys and generally helping. One of her fondest memories is of a month spent at their vacation ranch in Shasta County. "I never had anything like a real vacation before. It was wonderful. Dr. Nellie just relaxed and played like one of us. We had a good time, fishing and all." Trips to the country property remained an important relaxation throughout Dr. Nellie's life, and she fished, hunted and rode horseback well into her old age.

Freida remembers her as "a wonderful mother, devoted to those boys. I remember one time it was John's birthday and he said he wanted a cake with coconut, so Dr. Nellie said, 'Freida, we're going to bake a cake.' In those days you couldn't get coconut the way we do now. We went all over town looking for a coconut. We finally found one on Mission Street. We had to crack it open and grate it and . . . but that was a beautiful cake, I never will forget it.

"I met my husband at her place. His mother worked for Dr. Nellie, too. It was the end of World War I and he was coming home, so Dr. Nellie said, 'Let's go meet him,' so we took the streetcar down to the Ferry Building to meet the troopship."

The end of that war, in 1918, was the time of the flu epidemic, when Doctor Nellie became the heroic, almost mythic figure her older patients remember. "People were dropping in the streets, turning blue and falling down. We all had to wear masks and a bag of camphor around our necks. Everything smelled of camphor." Concurrent with the flu epidemic was the diphtheria epidemic, which killed half the children in some areas. Sometimes, with flu and diphtheria, whole families were wiped out. "Dr. Nellie never stopped; she was everywhere," Eloise Hugentobler says. "Sometimes she would come into my mother's boarding house worn out, and she'd sit down at the big dining room table and say, 'Mrs. Fon-Taine, I'll just sit and rest a minute and have a glass of your wine.' She was like one of the family."

There was no cure, only "Dr. Nellie coming by each day," as Manuel Piver says, "to see if my parents were still alive, take their temperature, try to make them comfortable. I was about eight. The lady next door was Mrs. Giovanetti. You know, Italians always had a pot of soup on the stove. She'd call me and give me a big pot of soup, and I'd feed them that. And whiskey. Everyone said whiskey was the only help. Or a little hot wine with sugar in it." Mildred Buzacott Adams was one of the lucky children who survived diphtheria. "I remember they gave me whiskey in milk, and Dr. Nellie would come and go, and my father sat by my bed day and night, watching me, reading to me."

From then on Dr. Nellie's office was always packed. She kept daily office hours but made no appointments. People came and waited their turn. They filled the waiting room; the overflow sat on the stairs. People who came an hour early, hoping to be first, found that dozens had preceded them. Often Dr. Nellie was late, out on an emergency or delivering a baby. "You'd go up there and wait and wait," says Betty Williams. "Then you'd hear her, pat-pat-pat running up the stairs. She'd call into the waiting room, 'I'll just go up and have a cup of tea, then I'll be right down.'"

Beyond the crowded waiting room was Dr. Nellie's examination room and office, a small room, informal, "like someone's kitchen." A huge, battered roll-top desk sat almost hidden under a clutter which nurse-receptionists were forbidden to straighten out, "...or I won't be able to find anything," warned Dr. Nellie. (This desk, cleared and visible, now dominates the living room of granddaughter Marion Null.) In those days simple urinalysis was done by the doctor. Dr. Nellie's patients remember being handed a white enamel pot and sent behind a screen to produce a specimen.

Everyone describes Dr. Nellie as a small, slender woman who wore a simple dress, longer than was fashionable, usually with a sweater over it. On housecalls she wore a long dark coat and always a hat. William Halloway remembers "the way she used to come into the flat we lived in. She would just throw her hat one way and coat another, and tell me what to do." Others say she was often too busy to remember to take off the hat. She might return to the office in a hurry and wear it all through office hours. Not that she was indifferent to her appearance. She was always clean and neat. She liked to have her hair tightly waved and sometimes complained, "Look at my hair!" when she hadn't time to go to the beauty shop. She wore glasses which slipped down her nose, and when she peered over them at people, they were never sure whether she was about to issue a stern order or crack a joke.

In 1925 Frank House worked after school in the drug store on the street level of the building. "She must have been about fifty then. The store was owned by Mr. Lomalino, who was pretty old and slow. You know, in those days, druggists made up the prescription right there, a pinch of this, so many drops of that. She'd come down there in a hurry for a prescription and she'd say, 'Oh, get out of the way, Lomie'—nobody else dared call him anything but Mr. Lomalino—and she'd make up the prescription herself and run back upstairs with it."

She was outspoken for a woman of those days, with an earthy sense of humor. One patient, worried that she might be pregnant, was examined and told, "Oh, no, and your ovaries are so high they'll have to hit the jackpot to catch you!" Another, lying on the delivery table, was praised with a sudden, "Look at those magnificent nipples!" her way of encouraging nursing mothers during the years when breastfeeding had become unfashionable. And when the joke was on her, she could take it. One patient teased her roughly, "So you let your husband get away from you?" Her quick retort was, "Oh, I got the best out of him first—I got my boys."

She now made house calls in a car, often driven by friends, patients, relatives she hired. Her nephew Boler Rucker, a state meat inspector, often stayed with his Aunt Nellie while inspecting slaughterhouses in Butchertown. "I drove her on calls. She went everywhere, sometimes to pretty rough parts of town. I'd worry, but she'd hop out of the car and say, 'Never mind, I'm safe.' One time she went into this place to deliver a baby, and came out and said to me, 'Go home and bring back sheets, towels...' a long list of things. The people didn't have anything, so she gave it to them. Of course, they couldn't pay her. Sometimes she'd come out of a house with her hands all wet and say, 'Well, the whole family is sick, so I just did the dishes and cleaned up a little before I left.' If she got a call in the middle of the night, she would drive herself. I remember I woke up one morning about seven when she was just coming back in, and she was all banged up and bruised. I asked her what happened and she said she had driven out to deliver a baby, but crossing Army Street she was hit by a truck. She climbed out of the wreck and went on to deliver the baby. She handed me a signed check and said, 'go buy me another car, I haven't got time.'" It was Boler Rucker who pointed out that the simple country doctor image or midwife image did not fit. "She went to bed right after dinner, where she'd sit up for at least two hours reading medical journals, keeping up. She delivered a lot of babies, but she did everything else too; she was known as a good surgeon."

Frances Anderton also drove for her, but usually only on Mondays, her day off. "Then we'd visit a friend, maybe drive down to Half Moon Bay or somewhere out in the country. We talked a lot. I took all my troubles to her, and she told me about her life on the farm when she was a girl."

Several patients told about being picked up by her and driven to the hospital. Evelyn Eleen's two-year-old sister Gloria needed a tonsillectomy "...but there was no money for it. Dr. Nellie picked her up, took her to the hospital, operated, and brought her home again. No charge." Clara Schmidt remembers the day her daughter Ruth was born. "Dr. Nellie came over early in the morning and said, 'I'll take you in the car for a ride and you tell me each time you get a pain.'" She rode with Dr. Nellie on house calls until it was time to go to the hospital.

Many babies were delivered at home, including my older sister. Dr. Nellie stayed with my mother during a prolonged labor, occasionally getting into bed with her, "...to comfort me. And she had your father assist during the birth. She said to him, 'You should be here to see what your wife goes through. It's just as much your business as it is hers.'" Other assistants at births were women she trained herself, often patients who showed some aptitude; she seemed to be always recruiting healers.

Elsie Orlando Collins remembers, "After I nursed my mother through pneumonia—making flaxseed tea and things like that, there was no penicillin in those days—Dr. Nellie said to me, 'You'd make a marvelous nurse, did you ever think about it?' I said yes, because in my heart that was what I wanted to be. But my dad didn't believe in educating women. So she said, 'When you get through high school, I want you to take the course at San Mateo Junior College, and if your dad won't finance you, I will.' I never took her up on it. Oh, I don't blame anyone. I could have somehow. And I'll always remember that she believed in me and would have helped me. She helped plenty of others."

Everyone I talked to mentioned money—Doctor Nellie's lack of interest in it. Her fees were lower than the average and often went unpaid. She was inconsistent about sending bills. Some people paid at the office. Many never paid. On house calls, she surveyed the situation and charged accordingly. Josephine Ganbini remembers the birth of her sister Loretta. "Doctor Nellie looked around at us four children—my Dad had left us, and now there was another mouth to feed—and she patted my mom's shoulder and said, 'Never mind my fee, buy food to feed the children.'" Some patients tried to show their gratitude by paying her in goods: a jug of homemade wine, food, linens. The wine was received graciously, then poured down the sink. Food and plain linens might go to needy patients. Fine needlework—afghans, patchwork quilts—have been passed down through the family.

One of the gifts of food which was kept and consumed heartily was Esther Binder's annual pound cake. In 1933 Esther's daughter Betty had been run over by a car. "Specialists operated on her four times. She was in a cast for thirteen months. Doctor Nellie came to see her every other day for months. She saw how hard it was, with the Depression, my husband bringing home little, and I was taking care of foster children, $17.50 a month from the county. I never saw a bill from her or from the orthopedic surgeons. For about a year I paid her ten or fifteen dollars a month, and when I got pregnant again, she said, 'You don't owe me any more.'

"So from then on, every year I made her a pound cake for her birthday, the eleventh of March. And she would say, 'You could give me a million dollars and I wouldn't be any more pleased than I am when you give me this cake,' except one time I made it with margarine and she made a face and told me sternly, 'Next time use butter.'"

In 1937 Doctor Nellie's sons completed their education, John at Stanford Medical School and Gilbert at University of California's Boalt Hall. Gilbert opened his law office in his mother's building, and John began medical practice with her. Now in her sixties, she began to refer patients to her son and talked about retiring. She certainly could have done so with honor. Iva Lannes suffered an emotional breakdown around that time. "I'd get out of bed and just fall over. Doctor Nellie couldn't seem to do much for me, so the family thought maybe she was getting too old and they called in another doctor. He looked at me and asked who my doctor was. When I told him, he said, 'Why did you call me? If she can't help you, I sure can't. There isn't anything she doesn't know. She's not just a doctor, she's an institution!'"

World War II made retirement impossible. Overnight Hunters Point became a major naval shipyard. "Temporary" housing projects covered the Hunters Point hills. Thousands of workers came from all over the United States, many of them black. During those days everyone left the classrooms, the offices, the hospitals, for the big money of the shipyards, and teenagers like my sister and me replaced them after school in medical offices. I know from my own experience that these offices opened their services very slowly and grudgingly to black patients. But according to Carol Rogers, one of the many women who worked at one time or another in the office, "Doctor Nellie never turned away a patient, never discriminated against anyone." And if, as her waiting room filled with black patients, some of her old patients deserted her, didn't this process simply follow the established pattern of her career? As people prospered, they moved away to higher priced neighborhoods near higher priced doctors, while Doctor Nellie remained in her building on Third Street.

In a letter dated 1960, the late Juanita Howell wrote to Doctor Nellie, "I came first to you for medical care back in 1944—almost penniless—ill—off my job as matron at the Hunters Point Shipyard, a widow with two children. You treated me, enabling me to go back to work, and cooperated with other doctors in the care of my little girl La Verne, helping to save her life. We all love you for all you have done for us through these years.''

La Verne Howell knew that her mother had brought her to California hoping that the mild climate would help her chances for survival, but she did not know at the time that the cause of her chronic weakness and pain was sickle cell anemia. ''My mother would take me to see Doctor Null. Now, I had been to doctors all my life, the Mayo Clinic, everywhere, and I was used to men in white coats and all. Here was this hunched up old lady in a housedress, her office desk covered with piles of stuff. She wasn't my idea of a doctor. Besides, I was a little scared of her, the way she'd look at me over those glasses of hers. But gradually I got used to her, and I could see that, with all that clutter and no white coat, she still knew what she was doing. She was gentle and caring. But she never smiled.''

By then, the early fifties, Doctor Nellie's strength was fading and she was worried about the deteriorating health of her son Gilbert. She stopped delivering babies or going on house calls, seeing only those people who insistently came to her office for emergency treatment, or for old time's sake. If she smiled little, she could still summon up a joke for an old patient in worse shape than she. May Dennehy remembers calling her about her aged mother, long bedridden and now sinking into depression. A former patient of Doctor Nellie, perhaps she would respond to her. ''Well,'' said Doctor Nellie, ''I can't drive anymore, but if you can come and get me, I'll see her.'' Then, at the bedside of the withdrawn old woman, she quipped, ''Mame, how come you still have your lovely skin, while I look like an old accordian?''

She was a bit short with the reporters who trooped up the stairs to her office in 1956 to interview her on her fiftieth anniversary in practice, when she was eighty-two. ''How many babies have you delivered?'' The same old question evoked the same old answer, that she had quit counting decades ago when she reached 5000. The phone rang constantly during the interview.

One comfort in those latter days was her four grandchildren: Gilbert, born in 1943, Barbara, 1947, Marion, 1950, and Patty, 1953. Marion Null remembers Thanksgiving Day dinners, ''. . . with lots of relatives. My grandmother cooked and baked pies. She liked to indulge my brother Gilbert. He loved whipped cream, so once she whipped him a whole bowl. He ate himself sick.

"Whenever we visited my father's office, we liked to play up there on the third floor. It had so many little rooms, nooks and crannies. And we slid down the bannister to the second floor, forbidden, of course, but we did it anyway. But I didn't like staying there at night; the noises frightened me." By the late fifties there were no more open fields. Traffic was heavy. And the entry and stairs where patients had formerly waited to get into the crowded waiting room had become an all too attractive shelter for late night street life.

"I don't remember much very clearly," says Marion. "You know how small children perceive adults—she seemed incredibly old to me, and stern, impatient. But I have one very clear memory of taking a walk with her. I must have been fairly young because she held my hand all the way as we walked down Third Street to go to the store. Every few steps we were stopped by people who wanted to say hello and pay their respects. Everyone on the street knew her. I was so proud."

In 1959 a stroke made Doctor Nellie's retirement definite and complete. After that she rarely left her upstairs rooms. Some of the women hired to care for her patients now came to nurse her. Her bed was moved into the living room, where she could rest frequently and still receive callers.

Esther Binder still brought her birthday pound cake and was pleased to see the afghan she had crocheted spread on the bed, while Dr. Nellie, now dressed in a house robe, made coffee for her and, for the first time, had time to sit and chat. Frances Anderton usually found her in bed when she called, but though her body was frail, her mind was as sharp as ever. Once, when Elsie Orlando Collins (who never did become a nurse) sat waiting at Gilbert's law office, Dr. Nellie came slowly down the stairs. They had not seen each other since the war. Doctor Nellie peered over her glasses and said, "Aren't you one of the Orlando girls?"

Marion Null recalls the last time she and the other grandchildren were brought to see her. "She was in bed. She couldn't talk anymore, but her eyes were clear and sharp. She took my brother's hand, held it in a strong grip, kept looking at him as if she was trying to say something, tell him something."

She died on New Year's Day 1964, two months short of her ninetieth birthday.

We don't need to idealize or sentimentalize Doctor Nellie Null or her times. No doubt her strong will sent ripples of conflict through her personal relationships. One person wrote to me with doubts about her judgment in one fatal emergency. And none of us wants to return to the days before children were immunized against diphtheria.

What we need and what we want to find in our lives is what she stood for: the ethic that placed all human beings above material gain; the good-humored gusto for life; the robust and unsentimental love that expressed itself in effective work; the inner freedom that makes possible a total commitment like hers.

In that sense we are, all of us, in search of Doctor Nellie.

* * *

The most recently written of the reviews included here appeared in the *San Francisco Chronicle* in 1983. I had read three books on Margaret Fuller and had struggled through some of her writing, which, outside of her letters, is clogged with learned allusions, probably intended to prove her erudite though female. I began to think of her as our New England George Sand, with no Paris near enough to run away to. When I heard that a complete edition of her letters was coming out, I had no trouble getting the two volumes for review. No authority had staked an earlier claim to them—Margaret Fuller remains only a name to most readers, even to many literary feminists.

After receiving the books, I almost gave up trying to write anything. They came late; I was given "at most ten days" to turn in a review of 800–900 words. I didn't see how I could read through two volumes of fully annotated letters, then write something which would not only comment on the letters but fill in some background on Fuller. Then I learned that these were only the first two volumes of a projected four. The second volume stopped at 1841, when Fuller went to New York and then to Europe. The most interesting letters were yet to come. I was at a loss about how to proceed, but I did not want to miss an opportunity to spread the word about Fuller and these fine books.

I gave up my attempt to read through all the letters. Instead I wrote a background piece on Fuller, with a few quotes from the letters. This is the only time I have ever "reviewed" a book without reading it.

The Letters of Margaret Fuller
edited by Robert Hudspeth

I do not ask or wish consolation—I wish to know and feel my pain, to investigate its nature and its source. . . .

I cannot promise you any limitless confidence, but I can promise that no timid caution, no haughty dread shall prevent my telling you the truth of my thoughts on any subject we may have in common.

(from the letters)

Unfortunately, we have not yet reached the day when a review of a book by or about Margaret Fuller can plunge directly into an evaluation of the text. First, the reviewer must review Fuller's life, for readers may know her only as the token woman in the Transcendentalist group led by Emerson. She was much more than that— in fact, much more than friends like Emerson could handle.

Margaret Fuller was born in Cambridge, Massachusetts in 1810. Her father educated her rigorously and, in the opinion of those times, inappropriately for a female, whose only proper career was marriage. She was twenty-three when he suddenly died, leaving her responsible for the education of six young siblings as well as for much of their support.

Despite penury, domestic demands, fragile health, and a passionately restless temperament, she accomplished much. She was the first editor of *The Dial,* the Trancendentalist literary magazine, for which she wrote the first really good literary criticism in America. An early feminist, she wrote *Woman in the Nineteenth Century* and conducted classes called "conversations," which offered literally the only opportunity for local women to discuss important issues freely. Horace Greeley hired her to write literary and drama criticism for his *New York Daily Tribune.* She wrote countless letters, some to men with whom she fell passionately in love; they all backed off and married less intense and challenging women.

At thirty-six she finally fulfilled her dream of going to Europe, where she met Angelo Ossoli, ten years her junior, an army officer at odds with his noble Italian family. Together they fought for the republican unification of Italy. She sent reports to the *Tribune,* hence becoming our first woman foreign correspondent. She bore Ossoli a son. The republicans lost. Margaret, Angelo and their infant had nowhere to go but back to America. On July 19, 1850, within sight of Long Island, their ship broke up in a storm, and all three drowned. Margaret Fuller was forty years old.

Emerson and others decided to put together her letters and articles and publish a book, her "Memoirs," as a tribute to their friend. With friends like them, she needed no enemies. These men simply could not deal with a woman who was both brilliant and passionate, who was simultaneously an intellectual, a romantic, a political activist, a feminist, and the adored lover and comrade of a young Italian rebel.

They cleaned up her act for her, obscuring details of the period relating to her "marriage," pruning her letters, "improving" them by substituting more lofty, ladylike words, and so on and on, until they produced a book which passed down to us the image of a priggish bluestocking whom subsequent biographers further trashed by implying that the intellectual lady was suddenly and finally "feminized" by her Latin lover. (A genteel, literary way of saying, "All that kind of woman really needs is a good _____.")

We now have books that give a clearer picture of her. For starters I recommend these: Paula Blanchard's biography, *Margaret Fuller: From Transcendentalism to Revolution; The Roman Years of Margaret Fuller* by Joseph Jay Deiss; Fuller's own *Woman in the 19th Century,* available in a Norten paperback; a selection from her writings edited by Perry Miller under the title *Margaret Fuller, American Romantic;* selections by Fuller and her contemporaries, *The Woman and the Myth,* edited and introduced by Bell Gale Chevigny.

And now we have these first two volumes of her collected letters, going up to 1841. Robert Hudspeth has taken exquisite care to restore existing letters as accurately as possible. Copious notes fill in the background, so that a leisurely reading becomes a complete course in the people and ideas of her time. Hudspeth has spent fourteen years on this project so far; I hope it doesn't take another fourteen to do the last nine years of letters, but if it does, they should be worth the wait.

* * *

I hardly ever write a negative review. Precious review space should be given to books which are worth writing about. If I don't like a book, I ignore it. I have written strongly critical reviews only when I felt an unworthy book or film had become so influential and so undeservedly popular that it needed to be deflated. That is what I did in "The New Cliches," and that is what I did in the following essay on Bruno Bettelheim's *The Uses of Enchantment.*

Since I was writing for a librarians' journal, I cited the page numbers of each quotation, which are, I believe, the same in all editions.

The editor of the journal, who had asked for my comments in 1980, five years after the book came out, then changed his plans for the theme of that issue. With publication date of the book so long past, there seemed no point in sending the review elsewhere; it was never published.

I print it here because as the years have passed, the necessity for deflation has grown. The book is used in so many courses and listed in so many bibliographies that a detailed warning against it is still needed.

The Abuses of Enchantment

During the 1950s, when my children were small, fairy tales had slid to low repute with many of the experts—psychologists who condemned them as violent and unrealistic. I continued to read and tell the old fairy tales to my children, compromising by skipping some of the violent endings. If any parents really abandoned fairy tales, I never knew one who did or who boycotted films like Disney's *Snow White.*

In 1975 Bruno Bettelheim published *The Uses of Enchantment,* which tells us fairy tales were really okay all along, in fact necessary to healthy development, even the gory parts. For the sake of today's young parents and teachers, I'm glad that fairy tales are "in" again and they needn't feel even a trace of bootlegger guilt or defiance while enjoying them with children. But I hope the popularity of this book over better analyses of folklore does not mean readers are absorbing, along with Bettelheim's reassurance, his limitations and prejudices.

His limitations as a reader of folklore and children's literature are severe. He extols the "folk fairy tale," by which he means stories in the oral tradition of Europe, later written down by authors like the Brothers Grimm. He does not acknowledge his omission of the vast body of non-European folklore, never mentioned except for a brief reference to the *Ramayana*. Nor does he trouble himself about the blurred lines between myth and folktale, confidently making dubious distinctions between them. He mistakenly places Hans Christian Andersen stories in both categories, and he demonstrates no knowledge of the variety of modern children's literature, which he mentions only in order to dismiss it.

His Freudian commentary on the tales is painful to anyone who loves literature, so predictable it reads almost like a parody of the form. Giants are the threatening father; wicked stepmothers are negative aspects of mother; Jack's beanstalk is masturbatory; conflicts are oedipal, with bits of sibling rivalry; leaving home means giving up oral fixation. Little Red Riding Hood picks flowers in obedience to her "pleasure-seeking id" until she remembers grandmother's warning, "the reality principle." And, of course, "to a child the greatest riddle is what sex is..." (129) Every story is reduced to a lock-step march of id, ego, super ego through oral, oedipal and genital stages. Doctor Bettelheim shows no sign of recognizing that folktales were told not only to children but to people of all ages, nor that people of all ages, even children, may have thoughts and dreams not covered by Freudian terms.

This narrow interpretation hints at a deeper rigidity, for which one example will serve. In a chapter subtitled "The Youngest Child As Simpleton," where Bettelheim discusses stories which give children hope of becoming more adequate, he rejects Andersen's "The Ugly Duckling" (mistakenly termed a myth) because "it misdirects his fantasy...His chance for success in life is not to grow into a being of a different nature as the duckling grows into a swan, but to acquire better qualities and to do better than others expect, being of the same nature as his parents and siblings...No need to accomplish anything is expressed...that one's fate is inexorable—a depressive world view—is...clear in "The Ugly Duckling." (105) At the very least, Bettelheim's reading of this story reveals grave deficiency in flexibility, in openness to the symbolic fantasy that he says comprises the value of fairy tales.

Does similar rigidity lead him to believe he can praise fairy tales only by dismissing other forms of literature? According to him, myths are too "pessimistic" (the example he cites is, of course,

Oedipus) and fables too didactic. Modern "realistic" stories are too "thin." His defense of "Little Red Riding Hood" as superior to "Little Tootle," the conformity allegory of the 1950s, is hardly necessary. But citing "Tootle" as representative of modern children's literature is cheating. The only other stories he mentions are another train story and *Swiss Family Robinson,* rejected because it offers "no hope." He take one brief swipe at the Bible; Cain and Abel don't help much with sibling rivalry!

He even attacks the literature of nonfiction and science for children, asserting that if given a scientific description of the solar system, "children come to distrust their own experience. . . the child needs to believe that this world is held firmly in place. Therefore he finds a better explanation in a myth (myths are okay here?) that tells him that the earth rests on a turtle or is held up by a giant." (49–50) Note that he is not referring to a two-year-old, but to "prepubertal" children. Thus his statement reads like an attack not only on the intelligence of children but on much of the standard elementary school curriculum.

This unnecessary dismissal of most children's literature exposes his ignorance of it and leads him into making extravagant claims for fairy tales. Every part of every fairy tale becomes a Freudian rite of passage, a symbolic aid in the child's psychic development. Even those violent revenges that the experts frowned upon thirty years ago are good because they assure the child that justice prevails in the world. Of course, it does not. Furthermore, revenge—at least in the best parts of our tradition—is not a synonym for justice. In any case, mightn't the child conclude that his or her own negative behavior would bring on torture and death instead of mercy, forgiveness, and a chance to do better?

Bettelheim's enthusiasm leads him to make promises, assumptions, and threats that surpass the fantasy of the tales he extols. "Many young people who today suddenly seek escape in drug-induced dreams, apprentice themselves to some guru. . . or who in some other fashion escape from reality. . . were prematurely pressed to view reality in an adult way." (51) In other words, an early dose of "Little Red Riding Hood" could act as antidote to the conditions which have produced the tragedies of drug addiction and Jonestown?

Even more disturbing is an attitude exemplified by Bettelheim's endorsement of the standard ending, "And they lived happily ever after," which ". . . does not for a moment fool the child that eternal

40

life is possible. But it does indicate that which alone can take the sting out of the narrow limits of our time on this earth: forming a truly satisfying bond to another." (10) In pronouncements like these, the author promises false solutions to great human problems like death and isolation, while at the same time ignoring the spiritual and religious, the transcendent element in folk tale and myth. In his hands "Cupid and Psyche" is reduced from the metamorphosis of the human soul through service to divine love, to a good sexual relation where "both partners. . . have a full life in the world, and with each other as equals." (295) As if such relationships were not constantly collapsing all around us under the weight of expectation that they could "take the sting out of the narrow limits of our time on earth."

These and other excerpts illustrate Bettelheim's blindness to the limitations of fairy tales. All of literature is limited by the perceptions of its creators, its audience, its time. Every story—even the most "realistic"—is a symbolic reach toward truth which more or less eludes our limited consciousness. Fairy tales and myth are indeed sources of deep psychic meaning. They are also sources of cruel stereotypes and misleading fantasies.

The hope for the arrival of a Prince Charming to give meaning to a woman's life is a long-standing fantasy which has blighted and embittered countless lives. The cruel stepmother is not only a negative part of mother, but a stereotype from which actual stepmothers have suffered. Snow White's wicked queen cannot "age gracefully and gain satisfaction from vicariously enjoying her daughter's blooming into a lovely girl" not because "Something must have happened to her in her past to make her vulnerable" (195) but because old women—in fairy tales as in real life—are seen as ugly, wicked witches, unloved, unwanted. And all the stories of simpletons and poor younger sons who find treasure, marry a princess, or conquer fierce monsters are passifying drugs to ease conformity to a life of boring drudgery.

Of course, the young man may be slaying monsters of his own psyche, and the royal marriage could be the powerful joining of one's masculine and feminine elements, and the treasure may be a spiritual one. Yet the prevalence of contemporary trash in romantic adventure books and films and the manufacture of real-life celebrity Cinderellas and politician princes indicate that transcending the literal acceptance of these fantasies does not automatically happen at the end of childhood.

We are faced with a difficult question. What parts of folktales or of any literature must be discarded because of sexist, ageist, racist, classist, conformist elements, and what parts may be kept and transcended through new interpretation? It is a question no one has satisfactorily answered. Bettelheim does not even admit that the question exists.

There is, finally, something about Doctor Bettelheim that his readers should never forget: he has swallowed the myth of the destructive parent, and has grown fat on it.

Contempt for parents is an occupational hazard for child and family therapists and teachers, sometimes mitigated by experience, age, and by struggling with the complications of rearing their own children. No such softening has come to Bettelheim. He holds to the classic Freudian premise that "Nothing is more important than the impact of parents and others who take care of the child. . . ." (14)

Thinking of average, normal children, we would be tempted to nod automatically. But Bettelheim's major work has been done "as an educator and therapist of severely disturbed children," and his reputation in this field is based on his work with the deepest and most intractable of childhood psychoses. In *The Empty Fortress* (1967) he wrote, "Throughout this book I state my belief that the precipitating factor in infantile autism is the parent's wish that his child should not exist." He dismisses the possibility of organic cause, despite the early onset of the disease in infancy, the uniformity of severe symptoms, and the presence of normal siblings reared in the same family. His claims of success in treating autism are questioned by others in the field who also question his refusal to submit his patients to diagnostic tests devised by them. (See Bernard Rimland's *Infantile Autism.*) One section of *The Empty Fortress* is the famous and frequently anthologized description of "Joey the Mechanical Boy." A passing reference to Joey in *The Uses of Enchantment* suggests that, unlike many of his colleagues, Bettelheim has not backed off from the parental rejection theory of autism.

Echoes of this unwavering indictment of parents for all the ills of their children reverberate throughout *The Uses of Enchantment.* Interpreting fairy tales in which characters give birth to changelings, part-animal children, he writes ". . . lack of control over emotions on the part of a parent creates a child who is a misfit." (71) He describes an actual father who told his daughter his own original Cinderella-type fantasies with the result that she ". . . lost contact with reality. . . and became schizophrenic." (127) Conversely he warns that "If a child is told only stories 'true to reality,'" the damage may be just as severe. "Many a child thus estranges himself from his inner life...he may later...escape entirely into a fantasy world, as if to make up for what was lost in childhood...This could imply a severe break with reality, with all the dangerous consequences for the individual and society." (65) So carried away is he by his theory of parental cause for all ills that he denies the objective reality of the world. "Maybe if more of our adolescents had been brought up on fairy tales, they would (unconsciously) remain aware of the fact that their conflict is not with the adult world, or society, but really only with their parents." (99)

To a psychologist capable of holding single-mindedly, through many years and experiences, to such a relentlessly exclusive theory, the only good parents are those who agree with him, admit what a danger they are to their child, and throw themselves on his mercy. Indeed his fame would indicate that a great many parents—seduced perhaps by his air of authority and by their hopes and fears for their children—have done so. But just in case there are some holdouts, parents who feel comparatively guiltless and competent, *The Uses of Enchantment* contains enough material to create the proper confusion, anxiety, and dependency among those parents educated and conscientious enough to wade through its analyses and proscriptions.

For it tells them that parents who make up their own stories, as well as those who stick to "realistic" books, may create a psychotic child or may plant the seeds for later adult psychosis. Parents whose adolescent is driven to drugs or cults may berate themselves for not administering enough fairy tales along with the vitamins and orthodontia, while reminding themselves that their teenager is not anxious about nuclear bombs, shrinking career choices, or chaos in sexual relations, but only needs to confront his conflict with them.

Even the parent-disciple of Bettelheim will find sticking to his advice hard going. For it is not enough to read fairy tales to children; the parent must do so with the proper attitude and belief in their value. Otherwise, "He won't be able to relate them in a way which would enrich the child's life." (118) Most conscientious parents could probably muster up the proper faith and enthusiasm even for the stories Bettelheim tells them portray monsters which are themselves in thin disguise. But they might glance anxiously at the child from time to time, looking for signs that the tale is useful in working through their child's "hatred" and "disgust" (124) for them.

43

Instructions on the manner of administering fairy tales encourage the telling of the story instead of "slavishly sticking" to written versions. (151) But Bettelheim adds a footnote telling about a father who stopped telling a story in the middle, leaving the child identifying with a perilous situation, his unconscious intention being revenge against the child's mother. Between this one and the father who drove his daughter into psychosis with his original stories, parents may wonder what enormities they are capable of, unaware, if they indulge themselves in telling their own versions of fairy tales with whatever embellishments occur to them out of the dark pit of their unconscious.

Even if a parent avoids these dangers and tells a story well, she or he must not immediately accede to the child's request for another, but must stop for discussion, because children need "ample time to reflect on the story." (59) And I always just let mine fall asleep! On the other hand, the parent must never explain a fairy tale to a child. This injunction should create no problem. I can't imagine that any parent would want to pass on to a child Bettelheim's rehash of the old Freudian explanation that Cinderella's foot fitting the glass slipper is really a penis entering a vagina. But I can imagine parents being made anxious about finding the correct, nonexplanatory answers to the child's questions about a story.

For the parent who nevertheless gets through all this with some confidence in knowing more about fairy tales and their "uses," Bettelheim has a final blow. "This is the tragedy of so much 'child psychology': its findings are correct and important, but do not benefit the child. . . adult understanding of the machinations of a child's mind often increases the gap between them." (120)

Ultimately, then, Doctor Bettelheim may be advising us not to read his book. But, of course, that part of his advice comes too late to be of use. Besides, some people may be required to do so for professional reasons, or may want to dip into the book for some interesting comparisons with other books on folklore. Readers should take what they can use from *The Uses of Enchantment* but should at all times remain wary of an author who announces with unblushing confidence that in his primary work, the treatment of severely disturbed children, ". . . my main task was to restore meaning to their lives." (4)

STORIES

These stories are printed approximately in the order in which they were written. "The New Sidewalk" (1961) is the only survivor of my early fiction efforts which is worth printing. "No End To It" was my first work of fiction to be published. It appeared in *Four Quarters,* published by La Salle College in Philadelphia in 1969. The other five stories were written in the mid-seventies. Four of them are printed here for the first time. "Something Coming" appeared in *Berkeley Poets Cooperative* in 1976.

The New Sidewalk

"No. I want it smooth." Louie Rocca thrust his belly forward and shook his head. "Smooth, like glass."

"Yeah, but you know, it gets a little wet from the rain, somebody's going to slip and break their neck."

"What's the matter? You can't do it smooth? You don't know how?"

The workman flushed. "Don't worry, mister. I'll make it like frosting on a cake." He inched his kneeboards further forward on the wet concrete. As he bent and reached for his trowel, I heard him mumble, "And I hope you fall on your fat ass some foggy morning."

I stood leaning on the wooden barricade with the other children and watched him work. His right arm smoothed the metal trowel back and forth over the thick gray ooze in a long sideways figure eight. Bubbles and swirls erased as he ironed them out in steady rhythmic movements.

"And you kids, you keep off it, see?" I jumped at the sound of Louie Rocca's voice behind me, and, as I turned, my nose almost hit his belly. I looked up at his face, trying to match his hard look with a defiant look of my own. I knew the other kids were watching, and Louie Rocca was our enemy. We never played ball in front of his house; if the ball went up over his roof to his back yard, he would keep it and say that would teach us to keep away from his property. There were so many children on the block that someone's father was always replacing a broken window. We had broken his window only once, and that time it had been his own son Dominic who was at bat. Dominic, to our surprise, had been terrified and had sworn on the Blessed Virgin that he hadn't done it; his father believed him and called us criminals, destroyers of property who would all end up in prison some day.

He pointed his finger at me. "First kid who touches it before it's dry, I'll use a two-by-four on him."

I moved away from him, but Roy stood still and stared back at him through his thick glasses. "Who's going to touch your lousy old sidewalk? Besides, my father says you touch me and he'll get the police on you."

"Hah. Sure, the police. They know you, huh, Roy? The young Mafia, that's what we got on this block."

He was right about the police knowing Roy. Roy's parents had never gotten over the surprise of becoming parents when they were nearly fifty years old. They shrugged in confusion as he ruled them and terrorized the neighborhood. Once he had thrown a lighted firecracker into our mailbox, starting an interesting, if small and quickly quenched, fire. The BB gun he received one Christmas turned him into the neighborhood sniper. The police had taken the gun from him, and he turned to knife throwing. An accident ended this phase before he managed to hurt anyone but himself. He had been practicing throwing his knife against a fence. The handle of the knife hit the fence, and the knife bounced back, hitting Roy in the left eye. Three operations had saved his sight, but he now wore thick glasses. The experience had not changed him, and the glasses, instead of making him look studious or vulnerable, only made his fierce eyes look bigger. No one ever called him four-eyes.

Louie Rocca turned away and began to walk around the wooden barricades as he had been doing since the concrete had been dumped.

For an hour he harassed the finisher, talking about pitch and drainage and joints while the man did his work. He smiled only when adults stopped to watch. Then he would point to the square in front of his house. No halfway patch jobs for him, he would say. Rip the whole thing out and do it right, he repeated over and over. His words implied an affluence rare in 1938, when the other fathers on the block were patching and painting only when necessary, counting themselves lucky to have met their last payment on the mortgage.

The adults would nod and walk on. We children were the only constant audience, and we gave all our attention to the workman, asking him questions and envying his being paid for enjoying such an orgy of mud molding. Finally he finished, cleaned his tools, and loaded them onto his truck, saying, "Just keep off of it till tomorrow."

Louie Rocca nodded impatiently and looked relieved as the man drove away. Then he turned and looked at the slick surface, delicately jointed in neat squares. Now it was all his. He owned the best sidewalk on the block. The other children had been called in to dinner, but Roy and I still leaned on the wooden barricade.

"What you waiting for? Go home. You kids go home."

I moved one foot, but Roy stood still, as if he had heard nothing. Louie Rocca moved closer. "You think I don't know why you hanging around? Soon as my back is turned you figure to write your name or some dirty thing on my sidewalk." He walked carefully across a plank to the front steps and sat down. "You might as well forget it; I'm going to sit right here and keep an eye on you."

Roy nudged me, and we turned and started walking slowly up the block.

"How long do you think he'll stay there?" I asked.

"I don't know. He can't sit there all night, can he?" Roy smiled. "See you later." He ran up the stairs and into his house.

I could hear my father washing in the bathroom as I walked into the kitchen. My mother turned from the stove.

"You're late. Dinner's ready. Wash your hands."

I washed my hands at the kitchen sink and dried them on a dishtowel. My father came into the kitchen and we sat down. My mother ladled pale yellow broth into our soup plates.

"I was watching the man put in the concrete," I explained.

"Is it finished?" asked my mother.

"Yes," said my father. "A nice job too. I saw it on my way home. Slick as glass." He laughed. "That guy don't know what he's letting himself in for. The way he hates the kids playing around his place. Why, when those kids see how smooth that is for roller skating, they're going to play all their hockey games right smack in front of his house."

I hadn't thought of that. Where had I left my skates? I began to eat faster. I wanted to suggest the hockey game to Roy before someone else got the idea—and the credit.

My mother sighed. "I don't know what that man has against the kids. It's a disgrace, a grown man yelling at them the way he does."

"He's a big bully, that's what."

"Eat your soup," said my mother.

"He likes to be the boss, all right," said my father. "He runs that house of his like he was Mussolini himself."

"And he gets to look like him more every day," said my mother. "His wife and the kids too. They're all round as barrels. Why, his wife told me he has a fit if they don't have pasta at every meal. I can cook as good as she . . ."

"Sure, you can. Sure."

"We don't prove anything by stuffing ourselves."

"He told me if you would fatten me up I wouldn't catch so many colds," I said.

"I guess I know how to feed my family without that big mouth telling me." The bowl of stew clattered as she set it down hard on the table.

"Take it easy," said my father.

"It makes me mad. All I ever hear from them is they got this and they got that. The only time they ever ask you into the house is to show you some new thing they got, and how they got such a good price because they know this guy and that guy, and you stand there and listen to all that big talk and they don't even offer you a chair and a glass of wine. You know all the time they haven't got any more than we have."

"He likes to be the big man, all right," said my father.

"Big man," said my mother. "I'm sick and tired of hearing what a big man he is. And how many acres he had in the old country. And how many men worked for him in the grape season. And how many rich people from Torino came to buy his wine. If he was such a big man, why didn't he stay there?"

"I heard it was his father's place," said my father. "And when he died, everything went to the oldest son. He and Louie didn't get along so well..."

"I can see why."

"...and he finally kicked Louie off the place. At least that's what I heard."

"Can I go out now, Mom?" I asked. "I'm finished."

"What about your homework?"

"No homework tonight."

"After the dishes. Just till it gets dark. Don't forget to put on a sweater. It's not summer anymore."

I hurried through the dishes while my mother put the leftover stew in the ice box and swept the kitchen floor. Louie Rocca probably was inside eating. I didn't want Roy to get to the concrete before I did. I hung the dishtowel on the rack, grabbed my sweater, and ran.

Some of the children were already playing one-foot-off-the-gutter, but I shook my head when they called me. I ran to the wooden barricade, where Roy was already standing.

Louie Rocca was still sitting on the steps. Next to him was a greasy plate with a fork and one or two strands of spaghetti on it, and a half filled glass of red wine. He had eaten his dinner on the steps. As I reached the wooden barricade, I saw something resting across his knees.

"That's right, kid. See? I got my shotgun here. I'm gonna shoot the first little bastard touches my sidewalk."

"You don't dare shoot me," said Roy.

"No?" He picked up the gun.

I pulled at Roy's arm. "Come on. Let's get in the game. I have to go in when the street lights go on." Roy let me pull him away, but he wouldn't play. He just sat on the curb until his mother called. As he waved good night, the street lights went on. Louie Rocca was still sitting on the steps holding the gun when I went into the house.

"He's got a shotgun," I told my mother as I undressed. "And he's going to sit there and watch. And anybody touches his sidewalk, he's going to shoot them dead."

"Did you hear that?" my mother said. "That crazy man. He's going to hurt someone."

51

My father did not answer, but I heard him open and close the front door. I got into bed and my mother turned off the light. In a little while I heard the front door open and close again, and I heard my father speak.

"It's all right. It isn't loaded. He showed me. But he says he's going to sit out there all night until the concrete is hard. He's afraid one of the kids will mess it up or a cat might walk across it or something. It's his business. Let's go to bed."

All night I dreamed of Louie Rocca. He was standing on his steps holding his shotgun. On each step behind him was a row of balls. One of the balls I recognized. It was the one I had lost over his roof a few weeks before. I was standing with sixteen other children, surrounding the fresh concrete. The wooden barricade was gone, and each of us had a toe touching the edge of the wet sidewalk. Roy was standing next to me. I looked down and saw that he was wearing roller skates. We began to chant, "Give us the ball, Louie, give us the ball."

He raised the gun with his right hand and with the other hand pointed to the balls. "I got fifty acres of the best grapes," he shouted. "Count them. Anybody tries to take one, I'll shoot him."

Roy crouched, then pushed himself forward. He spread out his arms and glided in a wide arc on one skate across the soft gray surface, cutting a deep track, and stopping in front of Louie Rocca. Louie raised the gun, pointed it at Roy, and pulled the trigger. From the gun oozed a string of greasy spaghetti which slid down the front of Louie's shirt. Then the balls began to roll down the steps. I looked at the sidewalk; it had turned into a sheet of glass. As the balls bounced down the steps, each one cracked the glass with a sharp clink, clink.

Clink, clink. The sound came from the kitchen. The edges of the window shades were light. I dressed as fast as I could, not stopping to tie my shoes.

"Where are you going?" asked my mother as I ran through the kitchen. "Breakfast isn't ready yet."

"I'll be right back." I ran out the front door. I was still half in my dream and almost believed that I would find glass in front of Louie Rocca's house. I ran down the front steps. As I reached the sidewalk I looked down the block and saw that there were, as in my dream, a group of children surrounding the square in front of the Rocca house. I looked for Roy, but he was not with them. Louie

Rocca was still sitting on his front steps with the shotgun across his knees. His head was resting against the bannister. He was asleep. With his eyes closed his face was softer. The thick cheeks seemed to sag and his mouth looked sad, as if he had unhappy dreams. None of the children moved. They were all watching Louie Rocca and seemed to be almost holding their breath.

When I reached the wooden barricade and looked down at the concrete, I saw why. Almost every inch of the new sidewalk was etched and lined. There were footprints in circles. There were pictures: a horse, a gun, a sailing ship, a house with a curl of smoke coming out of the chimney, a knife, a fire cracker exploding, a tree. Neatly lettered along the curb was the entire alphabet. Across the middle of the sidewalk, gouged in letters a foot high, were the words, LOUIE ROCCA IS A BIG FAT WOP.

No one said a word. As I turned to look at the faces of the other children, I saw Roy across the street, standing in front of his house. I called to him, "Roy, look." But he only smiled and went back into his house.

I heard a clattering noise and looked back. Louie must have heard me. He had moved, and the gun fell off his knees. As he opened his eyes, the children ran. I ran too.

Years later, Louie Rocca's sons replaced the concrete, but for as long as we lived there the sidewalk remained as it was. Neighbors averted their eyes as they passed it, and looked up or to the side if they had to walk over it. We children never mentioned it, even among ourselves. For a time we avoided Roy. Such a permanent symbol of public defeat was, I suppose, more than any of us had wanted. Perhaps we had some vague concept of fair play extending even to an enemy.

Roy and I drifted apart. He had taken to using his knife on whatever small animals he could capture. That and schoolwork began to absorb him and, I guess, led to his later success. He's a famous surgeon now, the only kid on the block, we often say, who ever amounted to anything.

No End to It

I don't see no end to it. I used to think by the time a man's fifty he seen everything. He's got a few things figured, you know. Like he gets peace and quiet to mow his lawn and have a couple of beers on a Sunday afternoon and watch the games on TV. That asking too much?

But everybody's going crazy. All upside down. My old lady says that's a sign I'm getting old, I can't keep up with the world. I tell her, it ain't like going to the beauty shop to get the latest hair style, like what's *in* this year. No. It's like, suppose you was playing a game, follow me? Learning, say, baseball. And you learn all the rules and you practice and you can hold your own pretty good. And then all of a sudden you go out there one day and everybody's doing something else, and you tell them, hey, you can't do it that way, that's against the rules. And they say, we didn't like them rules, so we're going to change them. And I figure, maybe they can change the rules, but then it's not baseball anymore. See what I mean? Never mind.

You take my son. When he's born I say to myself, you're a no-body with a fourth grade education, but your son is going to be somebody. Sure, I know, everybody says that the day his son is born. It's only natural to want something better for your kids. I start to think of all the things happened to me when I was a kid, all the crap I put up with, and I decide there's a long list of things my son ain't never going to have to see.

Like he's never going to be hungry. Or wear clothes two sizes too big so they last longer. And if someone says *rat* or *roach,* he's going to say, What's that? Or never share a bathroom, so you always know no matter how early you get in there, somebody already peed all over the seat. He's never going to start going down into the mines when he's twelve years old and start coughing his life away before he's thirty. And if he gets sick, I pick up the phone and call the doctor, right now, never mind the money. And he's not going to leave school and work for the rest of his life at some crummy job and never amount to anything. That was the big thing. Not only high school; you need a high school education just to dig a ditch. Right from the beginning, my old lady too, we was set on him going to college. That's why we only had the one, so we could do things for him.

You're going to say we spoiled him. Hell, we never could afford to spoil him. Things were rough after the war. We got out of that coal town and came here and I didn't even have a trade. Soon as I got into the plant, there was a strike, and we were out six weeks. That was the first big fight my old lady and me had. She was afraid; she said I should scab; but I says no, in the long run that's no good, we got to stand up for decent wages and the safety precautions. I was right, she admits it now, we got a health plan and all, but then it was rough; and I'll tell you one or two days there, Rick wasn't hungry, but me and the old lady was.

But we hung on, and we got our conditions, and I started making pretty good money. Every time our contract came up, we pushed hard, and we did pretty good for years, until automation and inflation and taxes and, well, that's another problem. I worked hard in the local, and I never tried to get out of picket duty the way most of the other guys did. I figured it was for Rick, so that some day I'd be able to send him to college. All the time he was little, we was getting him ready. The old lady, she used to read to him all the time and even taught *him* to read a little before he started school. How do you like that, little kindergarten kid, the book bigger than he was, reading. We took a picture. I still carry it, see?

And all the time we keep telling him, you're going to go to college so you'll be somebody. You don't have to be a nobody like your father, standing on a lousy assembly line all day, the noise so loud you can't hear yourself think, and nothing but this every day for the rest of your life. We started before he could even understand.

So he never even thought to ask, do I want to go to college? He was going, just like breathing.

Once, when he was about sixteen, he gave us a little scare. His best friend quit school, got a job, bought a car, all that. But I fixed it. I got Rick on at the plant temporary for the summer. A few weeks was enough. He said one day, how do you stand it, Pop? But I don't think about it anymore, like serving a sentence, a day at a time. I got ten years till I retire, and I figure my son is never going to count off the years like this; so what else could I ask?

About that time my old lady goes to work. She says it'll be better to start saving ahead a little for Rick's college, and besides she doesn't know what to do with herself in the house anymore. So she takes up typing and gets a job in an office. Besides, prices are going up, and it's like no matter how much we get for a raise, it ain't enough to keep up with the inflation, and we want to make sure there's enough money for Rick to stay in college so they won't take him in the army. That's another thing I don't want my son to see if he can help it; it wasn't like the old movies on TV.

There's no trouble getting him into college; he's right at the top of his class, he can take his pick. He wants to go back east to a place I never heard of, but he says it's very good, and he can make good connections there, so we send him. It should be good, it costs a mint, even with the scholarship he gets. Only thing is we can't keep paying plane fare for visits, so it gets lonely sometimes. At first everything is fine; the first year when he comes home for Christmas, he's going to major in business administration, and minor in English so he can go into advertising. I'm pretty proud of the kid. I take him everywhere that vacation, even to the plant, showing him off. It's like I just became a father again, passing out cigars and telling everyone what a fine son I got. He gets embarrassed. I think he's a little ashamed of me. Why shouldn't he? What am I? A nobody with a fourth grade education.

When he comes home in the summer, he wants to work at the plant to help out with his expenses. A good kid, you see, not spoiled. I look back on that time now, like it was the Garden of Eden, the best time of my life; it seems like years ago.

The second year the trouble starts. Not all at once, just little things you don't notice. He comes home for Christmas, very quiet, reads a lot. Says he's not so sure he wants to be in business. And I say, so change your mind, you can be a doctor or a lawyer, anything you want, I'm not going to tell you. He gives me a funny look and says, do I have to be a doctor or a lawyer. So I says, well what do you want? and he just shrugs. I know something's bugging the kid, but he's not talking. His mother can't get nothing out of him either.

When he goes back to school, he starts writing these long letters; they don't make any sense, and I even wonder, Jesus, I hope he's not taking anything. One of the letters says maybe he wants to be a teacher, and I even swallow that. I tell my old lady, write back and tell him, sure, why not; it don't pay any better than I make on the line, but it's clean work and plenty of vacation time. I wasn't trying to push the kid, you know? Then for a long time he don't write at all. We even call him a couple of times to see if he's all right, and he says, yeah, I'm all right, and that's all he says.

Come June, we go to the airport to meet him. I didn't know him. His mother almost passes out. You should see him. Hair down to here. Clothes like I wouldn't give to a tramp. I look at him and say, what happened, somebody steal your money and your clothes? He just looks at me, and the old lady pokes me to shut up and act like it's nothing. And we go home and she's talking and laughing, and Rick and me we just sit there and look at each other like across a gulch where it don't pay to talk because you're too far apart to hear what you're saying.

That night was bad. He goes to his room early, and we sit up, me saying is this what we worked so hard for and my old lady saying what did we do wrong? That kind of stuff, you know. Don't get you no place. So we both decide we're going to pretend he don't look like a mangy lion. So next morning I ask him, casual, how's school? And he says, he don't want to go back. It's like another kick in the gut. His mother drops the coffee pot, and we're all jumping around making sure no one's burned and cleaning up the mess. Then we sit down again all quiet, real quiet.

I don't see any purpose to it, he says. I don't know what I want to do. Just go to school, his mother says, find out later what you want to do. They'll take you in the army, I says. No, they won't, he says, cool as ice. I won't go. That's all we need. His mother starts crying, and that drives me almost crazy and I start yelling, "Did I work my ass off all these years so I could have a convict for a son?" And that's all the talking for that day.

Next day he says when does he go to work in the plant like last summer. I just look at him; then I say, let me understand you, you intending to work this summer? He says, sure. I says, where? At the plant, he says, real slow, like I'm dumb. And just as slow I say, looking like that, I wouldn't take you to the plant, even if they'd hire you, which they won't. And that's all the talk for a whole week. His mother tells me he's out every day looking for a job.

At the end of the week I come home from work and I hear the old lady singing in the kitchen. I walk in and she gives me a big kiss and she laughs. I figure he's finally driven her batty. Then she puts the food on the table, humming all the time, and she calls, Ricky, dinner's ready. And he comes out. Clipped. The beard is shaved off and his hair is short, well, not real short, a little dripping down his neck, but you can see his ears anyhow. I start to smile, but then I figure he'll think I'm crowing, so I just say, you look good. And he says, you were right; I couldn't get a job. And I say, "I'll take you down to the plant Monday." And I think we all feel a lot better. He goes out with some of his old friends that night, and the old lady and me talk it over and decide we won't push him about school. It'll be like before, a few weeks in the plant and he'll be ready to go back to college.

So that's what we do for the next month, and everything's going pretty good. I notice he's talking a lot to the guys at the plant, very friendly, but he complains same as ever about the work, so I think everything's going to work out. Except sometimes I see guys looking at us kind of funny when we come in the locker room. Then this old guy, Mike, comes up to me one day and says, you know you better muzzle that kid of yours. What's the matter? Well, he says, the kid's going around to all the guys telling them the union ain't looking out for them, and they ought to run the plant themselves, and, you know, the kind of stuff I ain't heard much since the thirties, about the working classes and all. The guys don't like it, the shop steward don't like it, the foreman don't—That's enough, I tell him, I'll handle it.

So that night I tell him, what're you trying to do, lose me my job? And he starts all this stuff like Mike said, with new words like military-industrial complex, and we just start yelling at each other, me trying to make him see that talking to these guys about anything but bread-and-butter is stupid and even if he made sense they'd call him a red and it would just make trouble for me, and was this all he learned at college? Then we stop yelling finally, and there's the big silence again. This time it lasts for the rest of the summer. He don't bother anybody at the plant anymore. He's polite at the dinner table, and every night he goes out. And his mother just looks miserable all the time, and I want to wring his neck.

Come September, one night, he says, look, I think I know what I want to do. I don't want to go back east again, I told you. I've applied to the university here, right here. I've been accepted. I can live at home. If you can pay the fees, I'll pay for books and extras out of what I made this summer, and Mom can quit work. Right away the old lady's crying again and kissing him. I could almost kiss him myself. I go out and buy him an old Chevy so he can commute easier.

And that's what he does. He goes to the university, and when I come home at night, he's there at dinner, and his mother humming around again, and after dinner he goes to his room and we hear him typing or he's quiet studying. It's a lot cheaper, but the old lady don't quit her job because things are already looking bad at the plant with the new contract coming up and the company making tough noises, and we figure she should hang on till we see how it comes out. Besides, she says, I like being out in the world where things are happening. What would I do at home? And I begin to relax, thinking everything's finally going to settle down. I'm thinking it was just a phase and he's all right again.

That's when the roof falls in. At first I don't know what's going on at that place except it sounds like a few jokers don't want to learn anything and don't want to let anyone else go to college. I say, if they don't like the school, they should quit and make room for others. Strike? They don't know the meaning of the word, and for what? They want to take over and tell the professors what to teach them. When I went to school, you kept your mouth shut and learned, or else they threw you out. That's all. If you're so smart you can tell the teachers what to teach, you're too smart to need school.

So, now, there's no more humming in the kitchen, just a big argument every night. Sure, he's with the strikers, what else? And he's explaining to me, like I'm some dummy, how the college perpetuates the system, and how the people who get the diploma get in and the others are out. And I tell him, I'm a nobody with no education, but I didn't need two years of college to learn that; I knew it since before you were born, why do you think I work my ass off to get you through college? Maybe if you went hungry like me and had to stand on that assembly line all your life, you'd be glad to go to school. And he says, that's just the point. And I say, You're throwing away everything we did for you, your mother and me, you're saying shit on it, and he says that's not true. And his mother just cries. And that's the way it is every night. No end to it.

And the students call a strike. And he goes out every morning at six o'clock to picket. And at six o'clock at night his mother and me sit and wait to see if he's going to come home or if we're going to see him on the six o'clock news getting busted. And I don't say anything to her, but I'm scared because I remember how bad things can get when you get tough on scabs and the police get scared and—but every night he's home for dinner, in the big silence, what is there to say? and then he goes out to a meeting. I'm so mad I could kill him, and I'm scared someone else will.

But I ain't got trouble enough. Contract negotiations break down, and our union goes out. This time it looks real bad. The company won't budge; right from the beginning they're hard-nosed like they can hold out forever. And half our members whining 'cause they're afraid they'll miss a payment on their new car, instead of seeing the long range loss if we don't hang together now.

So there we are, and I wonder if things can get any worse. At least we talk a little now, like the day the police used mace on the campus. I seen worse in the old days, and I told Rick a few stories I'd forgotten myself. It wasn't all chanting and sign carrying then, but I didn't tell him about how sometimes we had to carry weapons on the picket line—all I need is to give him ideas! And my old lady, she just comes home from work and gives us dinner and goes to bed while Rick and me each go to our meetings. Once we're talking again I try to get Rick to be sensible. Like maybe he should transfer to another college and I should quit the plant and see if I can find something else. And he says, in the long run, that's no good. If you don't stand and fight here, you just have to do it someplace else. Like he's been listening when I telephone the weak brothers at night and give them the old pep talk. And I don't see no end to it.

And I don't see how no good can come out of it. Except maybe what happened last week.

I was out on the picket line, as usual. It was raining, as usual; it always rains when I pull picket duty. And I was hunching up in my jacket, trying to sink my head in as far as I could and asking myself what kind of half-assed jerk I was, walking in the rain at my age, I'd probably die of pneumonia. And guys I never thought I'd see cross a picket line, going through.

Then I see Rick coming, and he's got about ten kids with him, three of them girls. He says, "Hi, Pop," to me and introduces all his friends, students from the university, strikers, and they all call me Sir and say how glad they are to know me, like good little kids when their mother says, be nice now and shake hands with your uncle, he's rich. Then Rick introduces them to the other pickets; he knows them all from last summer. Then he says to me, who's the picket captain, and I tell him, you know I am. And one of the other kids says, can you use us, Sir, we want to walk the line with you a while.

Well, I don't know how the other pickets are going to feel about these kids, they never had a good word for that strike, they say anybody can go to college has to have rocks in their heads to strike. But then old Mike, who's listening to all this with a funny smile on his face, says there's no rule against citizens joining a picket line, and we welcome any support we can get. So there we are with these ten kids mixed in. Pretty soon they start to talk and our younger pickets are flirting with the girls a little, and before you know it old Mike's teaching everybody to sing "Solidarity Forever." And I'm thinking, that's all we need, the next company press release will be about the conspiracy between us and anarchist students.

I manage to get next to Rick, and while we walk I ask him what's it all about? He says, when the kids heard about you being on strike they were impressed. I say why? And he says, well, their parents are doctors and lawyers, white collar people. They don't know anything. He says how he told them some stories I told him at dinner, and since they found out he was the son of a working man, they really look up to him. And I try to get it straight, but we're always interrupted, one kid after another asking me questions about strike tactics, and liaison between the students and the working classes, and I laugh at their half-baked schemes but they ask why I'm laughing, and they sure listen hard when I tell them. After a couple of hours everybody's cold and wet and just walking, and I'll hand it to these kids, they probably never had to walk to the grocery store in their lives, but none of them complains or tries to leave; they just hunch up like me and keep walking.

And then Rick and me are together again and I shake my head and tell him, your friends are not too bad, at least they listen respectfully to your old man. And he looks at me with this big smile and says, why not, you have something to tell them. You're somebody.

We didn't talk at all anymore. Tell you the truth, I couldn't. I had this lump in my throat.

Which don't mean I agree with him. I still think the kid's crazy. So every day we go out and picket and at night we sit at the table and argue. The old lady goes to bed, and we're still sitting at the table yelling at each other.

Only last night she don't go to bed. She says something a couple of times, I don't really hear, and then she yells at me, something about going on strike. Who? I says. And she says, the girls at the office. I been trying to tell you but you never listen. What strike, I says, you're not even organized. And she says they're getting organized. And Rick says, how can you go out on strike, you're the sole support of the family now. Then she's really mad, and slams down a dish, and says, oh, you're so pure but you want me to scab.

Then she tells us how some of the younger women (they got college degrees and they're still behind a typewriter just like her) have been trying to organize because they make less money than the men and the men get promoted to the top jobs where they make even more money for doing nothing while the women still do all the work. She tells how she never would have got the job to help pay for Rick's education if she hadn't come cheaper than a man; so that means she's been a scab right along. And then, get this, she says she's tired of working hard all day and coming home to fix dinner for a couple of lazy bums who won't even dry a dish or pick up their dirty socks. I never seen her so mad. And she didn't cry either. She just gets up and puts her coat on. I ask her, Where you going? and she says to a meeting, and on the way out she slams the front door.

So Rick and me do the dishes, both of us saying nothing, and finally he says, she's right. I'm so tired I just nod my head.

Then after a while I tell him, you know what I think. I think she's right. And I'm right. And you're right. And everybody's right. And I don't see no end to it.

Casualties

I hated high school.

My parents, who had left school at fifteen, were always saying these were the best years of my life, a statement that would have driven me to suicide if I'd believed it. But I'd have broken their hearts if I quit school, so I put in my time, served my sentence, as best I could. I was safe from violence because I was big, six foot three. I eased the boredom by reading constantly. And I embraced isolation because I despised adolescents, even though I was one.

I hated the anxious giggles of the ones so eager to be liked, and the slouch of the smokers on the corner, and the cheap sentiment for suicidal singers. Most of all, I hated the narrowness. My favorite teacher had been driven out, humiliated and bitter, because he was odd-looking, shy and sort of dreamy, the way really interesting people often are. Believe me, Socrates, with his pug nose and subtle questions, would never have made it in my high school.

No, the idol of my high school was Chip Barrett. Chip played football, wore the right clothes, had the prettiest girls, and murmured the right slang at exactly the right time. He smiled, smoked dope, and cut classes enough, but not too much. He showed daring only on the football field, behind the wheel of his car, or on the front steps where the in-crowd gathered. There, while clowning, he sometimes went a bit too far and started a scuffle that could easily have become one of our semiannual riots. Yet even in this he was consistent, showing merely the adolescent recklessness that passed for courage. He embodied the myth of the carefree teenager, as dreamed of by forgetful adults, as longed for by miserable teenagers. But to me Chip seemed like an actor trapped in one role, a prisoner of it. So I did not envy him. In fact, despite this detailed description, I seldom noticed him until the day I was forced to.

That day came just before Easter vacation, two days after my sixteenth birthday, at a rally which filled the auditorium with the entire student body of twenty-two hundred. As usual, there was some delay in getting the program started, and I did what I always did during the intervals of chaotic emptiness in every school day: I read. I remember that I was just starting Dostoevsky's *The Idiot*.

I sat about half-way back in the auditorium, on the left side. All around me kids were shouting at each other to be heard above the roar of others shouting, or jumping up and being waved at to sit down by teachers with eyes like shell-shock cases. I turned it all off, escaping into my book. Later, of course, I heard the full testimony of witnesses to what was happening in the balcony.

Chip was up there, sitting with two girls who were playing toy ukeleles. He started singing raunchy songs, and the kids egged him on. So he got up and did a mock south seas dance, a combination of a hula and a strip. Some kids in the back of the balcony started calling him fairy and throwing lighted matches at him. A couple of them shouted that they would make him do a real strip. He dared them to try, and that started a chase up and down the aisles, over chairs and people, all, I suppose, exciting Chip to more reckless performance.

They almost caught him near the front of the balcony, but he slipped out of their hands and jumped up onto the metal railing. Instantly everyone in the balcony froze as Chip began to walk the railing like a tight rope. He made it almost to the end, almost to the wall. Then, without any warning or any stumbling or slipping, he lost his footing and went over.

Chip wasn't killed in the fall. He wasn't hurt at all. Because he landed on me.

I was unconscious for about a week. Then came flashes of pain that spread into longer and longer agonies, dimmed by drugs. I suffered, therefore I would live. Gradually I knew more than pain and drugs, and the doctors told me I was very lucky, because my mind had returned completely. Whenever doctors tell you you're lucky, you can be sure there's bad news coming. The bad news was permanent paralysis of both legs, weakness in my left arm. The pain would gradually go away, they said. They were right about everything but the pain; it wanders but never goes away.

Once I had decided not to die, there was a lot to do: hydrotherapy, exercise, learning new and complicated ways to accomplish old, formerly simple acts, like sitting up, or washing my hair, or shitting. At times the small goals seemed hardly worth all the trouble, and I'd have to remind myself that this was it, this was what there was for me to do, if I was going to do anything. So I learned to cry without caring if a nurse saw me, then to swear, then to try again. Things were better when my vision cleared and I could read away the pain, just as I had always done.

My parents helped a lot once they got over the shock. My mother quickly learned what help I needed, and when I needed just to be let alone. My father came straight from work to sit with me every night for the two months I was in the hospital, and never let me know how much he was borrowing to pay for my care.

I had a lot of visitors too, at first, kids and teachers from school. People are funny about serious illness or injury. They hate to visit the victim, and they expect high payment for their sacrifice. They expect you to be brave, cheerful, uncomplaining and, above all, reassuring and grateful to them. It was exhausting. I had enough to do without cheering up my visitors, so I was relieved when they stopped coming.

Only one of the kids persisted in trying to visit me, and that was Chip Barrett. I told my parents to tell him I never wanted to see his stupid face; I'd kill him on sight. They agreed with me, though my mother bit her lip and murmured that she felt sorry for Chip's parents, she knew how she'd feel if . . .

"If I did something like that!" I was incensed that she could even imagine me capable of such a stupid trick.

They didn't mention Chip again until just before I was ready to leave the hospital. "He calls a couple of times a week, asking if he can see you for only a minute."

"I don't want to see the guy. Look, I don't even know him!"

My mother nodded. "I was just telling you because when you get home, he'll probably be calling..."

"Oh, shit, all right, let him come here, not home, here, just once, let's get it over with. But you tell him this, tell him if he comes in here and says, I'm sorry, and expects me to say, that's all right, he better not show up. I'm not dispensing forgiveness this week. Tell him."

The next day my new wheel chair arrived, and I started breaking it in, making tight turns between the bed and the window, loosening up a little stiffness in the right wheel. I finished a good, smooth turn, then looked up to see Chip standing in the doorway. I hardly recognized him. He was pale, and his face seemed pulled slightly off kilter from muscles tensing in ways they never had before. His clothes hung all wrong on him, and his hair stuck out in the wrong places.

"I brought you a book," he said, still standing in the doorway, until I nodded that he could step forward and hand it to me. It was a new study of the Greek myths, one of the books I'd put on a list for my parents to get. I nodded and threw the book onto the bed. Then I waited to hear what he would say.

"Nobody talks to me. They don't even look at me. They remember, you know, every time they look at me. And I can't, you know, fool around, it's like...dancing on somebody's grave. That's what Patty told me, you remember Patty. We broke up. She's going with Ojay Pierce now. And at home...my folks treat me like I was the one who...like I'm the cripple."

He went on that way for a while. He never said he was sorry or asked me to forgive him or asked how I was feeling or if there was anything he could do (I had an answer all ready for that one) or said any of the things I expected him to say. He showed no sign of a stricken conscience, no sign of any moral sense at all. His world had been changed, and he was describing the change to the one person he knew who could understand what this kind of change meant, this blow from outside. He—and I—had suffered...an accident. He had not yet even made any connection between his actions and their results. It was amazing how thoughtless he really was. But

68

here was the painful beginning of something like thought, something from inside, from the real person sleeping inside this former teenage hero. I was interested. I think it was the first time since I regained consciousness that I felt spontaneously curious, and curiosity is a great painkiller.

The day I came home from the hospital Chip showed up again. I was very tired, but restless and hurting. He stood there for a minute, then picked up the book he'd given me and started reading it aloud until I dozed off. The next day I read aloud to him from the second chapter. I don't think he understood what he heard, but he listened. The moment I became tired he knew, and he left. The next day I started teaching him to play chess and was surprised at how quickly he learned the moves. The next day he took me out and pushed me around the block a couple of times.

Each time he came after that, and he seldom missed a day, he learned something new about my exercises or my needs, and he helped me with them. He was stronger than my mother and handled me more easily. He seemed to know what I felt or needed almost before I did.

"You're pretty good at this. Maybe you should become a doctor." Even before he shook his head and made a joke about not being smart enough or studious enough, I knew I was wrong. "A healer then, a kind of nurse." He was pleased.

My parents were not. They were astonished that a friendship seemed to be growing. My mother was a little jealous, I think, because he was doing many things for me that she used to do.

"I though you said you didn't want to allow him the luxury of doing penance."

"I don't think it is penance for him," I explained. "He just has nowhere else to go. Like me."

"And when he has somewhere else. . .?"

"Why, then he'll go, I guess."

"Then. . .you like him?"

I thought about that. "I think there must be a lot that's likeable inside him," I said cautiously. Actually I didn't understand my relationship with Chip either. Looking back, I'd say the accident had changed my life but not my nature, my way of looking at things. I had been so tight, so self-contained, so closed against my uncongenial surroundings, that I'd been in danger of closing off everything, everyone. My injury could have finished me off, buried me.

Chip was my only line to the outside. And, I am convinced, I was a line to the inner self he needed to find.

During his visits Chip did most of the talking. He talked about concrete things, incidents, people, news events, all immediate, nothing from the past or the future. I found his talk soothing. We played chess. He took me out in his car. He massaged my weak arm and helped me exercise. He entertained me with pointless, good-humored jokes. When I was tired, he read aloud to me. When I felt better, I read aloud to him, explaining and commenting on the book. Sometimes I even read to him from my journal. He liked that best, especially my descriptions of clouds or trees or birds I saw from my window.

Toward the end of the summer he told me that he dreaded going back to school.

"Don't worry, everyone has forgotten over the summer."

"I haven't." And there it was, filling that smooth face, the first sign of responsibility: guilt. It's a rotten thing, guilt, but sometimes it's the first glimmer of better possibilities.

"Shit, as if I'd let you!" I said, and I laughed. Then he looked me in the eyes and laughed. Then we were silent together, and I felt a great weight slide away from me. I'd forgiven him.

That night my parents told me they were going to sue the school board.

"What do you mean, what for?"

"For a million dollars," said my father. "The lawyer says we can get it."

"But for what? On what grounds are you going to sue?"

"There was no teacher up in the balcony."

I nodded. "Old Mrs. Samuels is usually up there, but she goes out for a smoke now and then. You would too if you had to sit there with those..."

"The lawyer says that's grounds for negligence. The school did not provide adequate supervision."

"Supervision? It's not a nursery school. How are a few teachers going to stop two thousand people if they want to riot or burn down the school or any..."

"We're not talking about riots. We're talking about one boy who..." My mother stopped. She still couldn't talk about it. "I don't understand why you're so angry."

"Because it's a lie...it's...what about insurance? The school is insured."

70

My father shook his head. "Some technicality. The insurance doesn't cover it."

"And there's no point in suing Chip's family," said my mother. "All they have is mortgages, a few thousand in the bank. Even if we took everything they had, it wouldn't be enough to cover your first week in the hosptial, let alone what you're going to need."

"Why sue them for what Chip did!" I was furious that they'd considered it.

"Someone has to pay."

After a long silence, my father said, "This seems the only way. But if you don't want us to. . ."

"Then you'll lose everything and be in debt for the rest of your lives." I shook my head. "I just didn't think about it."

"Don't think about it," said my mother. "All you have to think about is getting strong. The rest is up to us."

When school started, Chip had classes all day and football practice until dark. I was busy too, preparing to take a test so that I could get into college on a special permit in the spring. Chip still came about once a week to play chess. Sometimes I helped him with his homework. He talked more often about the future now, doubting that he should go to college right after graduation, saying he thought he needed at least a year to work, "to do something real," instead of just moving on to more classrooms, more football.

"How are things at school?" I asked him.

"Not bad."

"Everyone has forgotten?"

He shook his head. "But they look at me, anyway. They're friendly, almost like before."

"Everything goes on the same," I said.

He nodded, then frowned. "Yeah, same dumb place."

Our court date came in December. Our lawyer had demanded a jury trial and insisted that I be there, even though I would not be called to testify. "You don't have to say a word, just be there." I think my parents must have told him what I'd said, and he had no intention of letting me say it in court. I asked him how long I had to be on exhibition like a freak. "Two or three days." And I couldn't even bring a book.

On the morning of the trial he made us wait in another room until the last minute. Then he wheeled me into the courtroom with my parents following. He got just the effect he wanted. The jury looked at me, then turned away, then slid their eyes back to stare at me. The principal and two teachers were there with the school lawyer. They looked shamed and confused and irritated, not sure whether to answer when I nodded at them.

Then an amazing thing happened. The door opened and in walked Chip, along with two girls and three boys. They took seats in the back row. The boys wore their team jackets. The two girls were cheerleaders, and one of them had just won a local beauty contest. All six looked fresh, bursting with youth and health, especially Chip, who had filled out during the summer. They sat quietly, soberly, respectfully. I smiled and raised my good hand at Chip; he grinned and nodded.

When I turned back, I saw that the jury's heads had all turned toward the back row, their faces relaxed with pleasure. There was no turning away, no sneaking of covert glances. What they looked at was not pitiable or ugly. It was youth's golden glow, personified in those six kids.

Later I asked my lawyer if he had arranged this too, for it seemed to me that if the jury leaned toward our side as soon as they saw me, it was sympathy for Chip that really won my case. He said, no, it was just a lucky accident that Chip had decided to attend. Neither side had subpoenaed him because the effect of his presence would have been unpredictable.

The trial took two days and part of a third. It was a great bore, and I couldn't keep my mind on it no matter how hard I tried. I'd already heard all that the doctors had to say about me, and my lawyer's assertions of negligence were wordy and pretentious, like most lies. The only dramatic part came when he put poor old Mrs. Samuels on the stand and made her cry.

I expected to be more interested when the school lawyer began his arguments, but his defense was dispirited, almost perfunctory. Maybe he was seeing the same thing that I saw: the jury. They seemed as bored as I with the testimony. Their eyes drifted first to me and then to the group in the back row, and their thoughts were easy to read. They saw me, my body broken and needing expensive care for the next fifty years. Then they saw the beautiful, glowing group in the back row, at its center Chip, still strong and healthy, with all his life before him. At the beginning of the first recess, when Chip and his group gathered around my chair to say hello, I saw one of the jurors brush away a tear.

I think the jury tried to do the right thing, probably what I would have done in their place. They found in our favor but cut the judgment to half a million. And by the time the verdict came, I was beginning to think that the responsibility, after all, belonged to the school board and the whole community behind it. They had imprisoned us in that place, had created our adolescence, with all its murderous folly, of which I was only the most dramatic casualty. Let them pay.

But I wasn't prepared for what happened when the verdict was read. The meek little group in the back row exploded. The girls squealed and the boys slapped their thighs, and they all jumped up to celebrate. But they did not turn toward me. Their joy was for Chip. They hugged him, kissed him, and Chip stood there, his eyes glazed and his mouth sagging with relief.

Then I realized that they did not see the verdict as I did, merely as a way of getting money for me. They saw it as a vindication of Chip. They took it literally and believed it. They believed that the trial had proven Chip not responsible. Innocent. They did not look once in my direction, but threw their arms around Chip and stumbled out into the hall. I could hear them beginning to sing.

I turned back to look at the jury and saw some of them smile and shrug. Only one of them even glanced at me, then turned away quickly, as if something in my expression had frightened her. Then Mrs. Samuels came up to me, and I was busy reassuring her that I didn't and never had blamed her for what happened. As soon as I could, I hissed at my parents to get me out of there.

I never saw Chip again. He had regained his hero status and was, if anything, more popular than before. I couldn't blame him for slipping back into that mindless, mirror-like state. I couldn't blame him for accepting what everyone else believed. I didn't even blame him for keeping away from me, who might only dredge up some jagged questions that had dozed off again inside him. The only thing I regret is that those questions never quite woke up in him, and never will, never can again.

Chip graduated and went directly to a small college with a big football schedule. He joined a fraternity with a reputation for pledging the most popular men and giving the wildest parties. In his second year he was killed at one of those parties, in the driveway of the fraternity house where he lay drunk, run over by an even drunker frat brother, his best friend, who was wheeling and screeching a stolen car round and round the house.

The friend who killed him was never charged with any crime, never even named in the newspaper. It was all referred to vaguely as an accident, described almost as a natural catastrophe, like an earthquake. The frat house closed for a while, and its members scattered to other colleges. But I understand it is now flourishing again, with much of its old spirit revived.

Three years after I finished college, I became a teacher in a high school, the first seriously disabled person to be hired, finally, for this one of nearly two hundred jobs I'd applied for, struggled for, screamed for. I still despise adolescence, but I can't help loving some of these kids, and I think I'm good for them, if only because I'm different. I used to be like the Ancient Mariner, telling them the story of my injury and Chip's death over and over. But gradually I came to see that they didn't understand, they thought I was criticizing *them,* just nagging them to be more careful. They weren't able to grasp the point of it all. So now, when the kids ask, I just tell them I was wounded in the war.

Something Coming

George, of course, just yelled when he found out. Forgot his arthritis and swung in here, right past the nurses, stood over me and started yelling. "I'll be broke, in debt, in disgrace. You did it, and I'll pay the price."

As usual he couldn't see anything but his own problem. I told him, life is full of surprises, most of them unpleasant. When I married you, fourteen years older than I, everyone said I'd be left a lonely old widow some day. But the things you worry about never happen. Other things do.

"Revenge! You never forgave me for Emmy, even though that was fifteen years ago and I never saw her again!"

Revenge? That's silly. How did I know I was going to die of cancer at forty-nine. If I hadn't gotten sick, no one would have known, least of all you, George. You'd have died happy in a few more years, content in knowing I'd give you a fine funeral. As for Emmy, I've probably missed her more than you have. She was my friend, after all.

He started yelling again. The nurse came in and said he'd have to quiet down; he was disturbing the other patients. Not a word about disturbing me. And she never looks me in the eye. None of them do. That's how I knew before the doctor told me. The minute I woke up from the surgery, the way the nurse in the recovery room looked at me, I knew I was a dead woman.

"I don't know you," he said, a little quieter. "Married thirty-one years, and I never knew you."

That's not news to me. I used to say it to myself at least once every day of those thirty-one years. What made me sad was that you thought you did. Everybody thought they did, as if there wasn't much to know. I started thinking so too. Until these last few years when I knew there was more than...oh, well, no hard feelings. Probably two people couldn't live together for thirty-one years if they really knew each other.

"How could you do this to me!"

George, I didn't do anything to you. When you think about it, you'll realize your perspective's all wrong. To me, it seems that you got all the benefits, none of the trouble. I shared all the money with you and none of the disgrace. Nobody's going to make you pay it back. They'll feel sorry for you. Because of your reduced standard of living. So you got a free ride. Early retirement and travel, and the Tahoe cabin (yes, that's mortgaged too, no equity at all) and the season tickets and the Mercedes (you're getting too old to drive anyway). You know I never cared about things like that. It was you who always talked about going to Tahiti. So I gave you the whole South Pacific with Japan thrown in for good measure. I never really enjoyed it. I'd have been just as happy staying right at home here in Berkeley, if it hadn't changed so no decent person could be happy here.

So then he kind of sagged and winced as he bent his knees and sat down. He looked down at the floor and started sighing the way he did the time our daughter announced she was having a baby. A black baby. As usual he gave up, sitting and sighing, and I had to make the abortion arrangements because I knew Susie just wanted to scare us again and didn't have any intention of getting saddled with a baby, black or white. But sigh as he will, there's nothing I can do about it this time. Dying is full time, and I can't take time out to worry about him. He's already had fourteen more years than I'm going to have, and maybe a lot more. Thin years, granted. But alive. If I were him, I wouldn't waste a minute of them yelling at me.

Finally he got up and said he couldn't forgive me for what I'd done. "But I won't leave you to die alone."

Alone, I told him, is the only way anyone dies. I was just mentioning something I'd learned, now that I'm an authority, just giving information. But he was offended and looked as if he might start yelling again, so I closed my eyes.

After he left, Susie called. I guess he must have let her know. I can't think how. Most of the time the phone is disconnected, like the plumbing and the people, at that communal slum, that holy farm where this year she is growing wormy potatoes and meditating. I haven't seen her since our thirtieth wedding anniversary party at the Claremont Hotel, for which occasion she showed up to greet our four hundred guests with her head shaved. Now there's revenge, if George wants to consider revenge. She has been relentlessly revenging herself on us since she was thirteen. Why? I stopped asking why about her or anything else, a long time ago. But now I have at least the answer to the question, how do you get a friendly phone call from your twenty-eight-year-old daughter? Drop dead. I was afraid she would want to help me die in the benefits of her new religion, but as it turned out, she didn't mention that at all.

"How'd you do it, Mom?"

Do what? Oh, the money. I just borrowed. You know all the old houses people left when Berkeley changed, and they moved out and rented them to groups of people like...like you and your friends. I started managing them, as a favor to old clients and friends who don't exactly relish dealing with a certain type of tenant. They were all free and clear. I mortgaged them.

"You forged the owner's signature?"

And then there were some who gave me money to invest for them. Without a note, that's right. People who've known me, dealt with me since you were in diapers. Who knows more about property and investments in Berkeley?

"And nobody ever suspected..."

What was there to suspect? I was keeping up the payments on all the loans, giving twelve percent on the money people gave me to invest. Everybody was happy. If I hadn't gotten sick...

"As simple as that?" A new tone in Susie's voice. Not only lack of hate. Respect? As if for the first time since I helped her with her multiplication tables, I had given her some useful information. "Is it that easy?"

For me. It wouldn't work for you, or for your friends. You have to be a stable person, with a business built over a lifetime. A respectable person, not allergic to putting in hours and hours, every day for years. With courtesy, good manners, proper dress. Oh, you don't know what I'm talking about. No decent person in this town would question a signature on a contract I brought in. But it takes the best years of your life to build trust like that. And I gave them. So my word was enough. For ten years I was chairman of the Ethics Committee of the real estate board.

She started laughing, and that didn't bother me because from my new point of view I see the irony of many things, my life among them. I would have laughed with her for the first time in fifteen years if I didn't know that any move would wake up the pain sleeping under the last hypo the nurse gave me. Then she sounded as if her laugh would end, and she was going to say something I've waited years to hear, but I suddenly felt afraid of hearing because it would wake up even deeper pain. So I asked her if she planned to come to my funeral naked, and in the middle of that laugh, I hung up.

I closed my eyes again and thought about the minister's visit and the way he just ran on nervously until I asked him if George hadn't told him what I'd done. "Yes," he said, "but my concern is with your immortal soul, not with money." I'd warned them they were hiring a radical when they got this new young man. They'll see. Anyone who'll dismiss money that way will soon have guitars and incense, like all the others.

We prayed for a while, and then he stood up, took my hand, and said, "I'm sure people will remember you only for all the good you did." I'm sure he meant to comfort me, but he made me feel just the opposite. Maybe with his attitude and George's fear of disgrace and Brenda's fear for the business, the whole thing will just be hushed up. I never thought about that before. I never thought of whether I would or wouldn't want people to know, after I'm gone. For so long it was my special secret. The excitement of knowing, even the bit of fear of what would happen if they found out. And the fun of dropping hints nobody ever picked up because I was above suspicion. That was more than the money. I never cared about the money. But after I'm dead, they should know. Give credit where credit is due.

Brenda came again this afternoon, faithful as ever. Twenty years we worked together, talked together, drank together. Many times she told me, when her husband died she would have killed herself if it hadn't been for me. She was the one who put me up for the Ethics Committee. I told her, listen, Brenda, we always wore the same size, and I've got that new two-hundred-dollar pant suit. You take it before I'm gone and George's sisters descend on the place.

She shook her head and took out a piece of paper and a pen. "So far we've traced seventeen of them. Here are the names. Now, which ones don't we know?"

I closed my eyes again.

Brenda started to cry, and I really did feel sorry. She's not young anymore, and this was a big shock to her. She smelled of scotch every time she came, even in the morning. I told her yesterday if she keeps this up, she won't last much longer after I go. Who'll nag her about her drinking after I'm gone? I like Brenda. But she's not very bright. I thought she'd never catch on. Every day she'd call the hospital, asking, "Shall I call Gleason? Their loan payment hasn't come in and it's already the tenth." And I'd tell her, don't worry, they're not a bunch of damned hippies, don't bother them, they'll pay. I knew it would all come out now, and maybe I should have broken the news to Brenda myself. But I'd just heard my own bad news, and I was too busy thinking about that.

"Why don't you tell me about the others?"

I felt too tired to open my eyes. Why hurry? She'll find out anyway, one at a time, when the rest of them call. Maybe some of them won't. Maybe old friends, for George's sake. And what's a few thousand to them anyway? Some of them, for old time's sake, might just pay off the loan and keep quiet. Some will just write off what they gave me, ashamed to mention they gave me money without a note. Oh. I wonder if someone might just step forward and pretend they gave me money, trying to collect. Now, I call that dishonest. At least I was paying back.

"You never thought about being sent to prison?"

I just kept my eyes closed and shook my head. And though I meant to say nothing, I found myself telling Brenda about that little mouse who worked in George's office. She did everything but brush his teeth for him, and he called her Miss Indispensible, and she'd blush and squint behind her glasses and scurry back behind her desk. She took over a hundred a month out of petty cash for more than ten years before he caught her. Cornered, she brazened it out, saying she hadn't had a raise for fifteen years, and she just took what was coming to her. She didn't go to prison. George just fired her and then complained he could never find anyone as efficient.

I opened my eyes to see if Brenda got the point. But she was just looking at me like I was crazy as well as dead. So I didn't tell her what I was feeling, that no matter how much more I made than

Miss Indispensible, I always felt the same way: I had something coming to me, and when was it finally going to come?

No, they wouldn't send me to prison, I told Brenda. Even if I was going to live long enough. Why, at my trial there'd be dozens of character witnesses. All the good I've done for this city all my life, the committees I worked on, the candidates I helped elect, at least back before the radicals took over everything. And the contributions. They'd be amazed how much of that money I gave to charity. What was I going to do with it? We couldn't travel much anymore what with George's arthritis and my having to keep my eye on all the payments. And what can you do with money except buy dinners you can't eat anymore, shows that give you a headache, clothes you'll never wear out.

Brenda had started crying again, when the door opened and the Gleasons marched in. I knew they'd show up. Most of the others would be ashamed to bother a dying woman, but not them. Frank and Abigail Gleason. Over thirty-eight thousand. Not that they can't afford it. Didn't I sell them four apartment houses in Alameda where there aren't any tenants' unions or trouble about keeping out blacks and long-hairs? And managed it all myself, for old time's sake, without charging them a dime. So I did mortgage one of them...two? Anyway, the others are still free and clear and bringing in good rents. They won't live forever. And they won't find anyone to manage their apartments as well as I did.

Frank looked stern and dignified, aloof, the way he has ever since he went deaf. Abigail was twitching around the mouth, but she was always too much of a lady to make direct complaints, so for a while they both just sat there, looking across the room about a foot above my body stretched out there between them. Old, old Berkeley, the two of them, as opposed to just old Berkeley, lying here dying of cancer at forty-nine. I used to wonder if my hair would turn as white-white as Abigail's some day, and then would I blue it and lean on my ornamented cane and talk of the days at Anna Head School before it dissolved with all the other decent values and places. Of course, Abigail always acted as if the school had gone pretty far downhill before I went there, but, still, she gave me a look that said an old Anna Head girl couldn't have done what I did.

Then she finally got out one word. "Why?"

And all of a sudden, even with my eyes still open, all I could see was that black boy we caught carrying out our color television. We didn't know what to do. He looked only about thirteen, and we didn't want to call the police. George held on to him, shaking him and yelling. But I tried to look at him in a kindly way. I asked him, why?

That dark, furious look he turned on me. I never forgot it. Then he said, "I wanted it." And I could see he was lying, or maybe he didn't know why. So then we called the police, but he didn't go to prison either, was only put on probation, because there's no room to put him and all the others like him and Miss Indispensible, all the ones who know there's something they've got coming, but it never comes, and besides, they really don't know what it is.

So I just looked at Abigail and said the same thing.

I wanted it.

Then I stared her down till she got up and marched out. That's the only way to talk to people who ask, why? Everyone who asks, why, is lying too, but won't admit it. I don't have to ask or wonder why because pretty soon I'll know everything. That's what the minister said. I hope he's wrong.

Backlash

"You have the right to remain silent. Anything you say can and will be used againt you in a court of law. You have the right to talk to a lawyer and have him present with you while you are being questioned. If you cannot afford to hire a lawyer, one will be appointed to represent you before any questioning, if you wish one."

The policeman read from a small card he had taken out of his shirt pocket. When he finished, he looked at Martin, then at the other guy, like an impatient teacher making sure his students were listening. Martin was able to return his cool gaze without so much as a twitch or a blink. It wasn't really so hard. He'd had years more practice than this kid in uniform. He cleared his throat. Keeping his voice steady might be more of a challenge.

"These aren't necessary," said Martin, looking down at the handcuffs holding his arms awkwardly parallel. He tried to pull his hands up into a more natural position, resting his elbows on his hips, but the handcuffs pulled and dug into his wrists. He let his arms fall again, feeling his palms turn up and outward in a supplicating pose he hadn't intended.

The policeman pulled out a book and a pen and began turning pages slowly, giving no sign that he had even heard Martin's protest. It didn't seem fair that he should handcuff both of them. Martin hadn't even moved when the other guy tried to get away. But the policeman had put cuffs on him too, growling, "That adds a 148, resisting, to the 647d and 288a. Felony 288a, you know." He spoke in a code that he seemed to assume Martin knew, as if he were arrested every day.

"Your name? Any ID with you?"

"In my back pocket," said Martin, and let the policeman reach for his wallet.

"Martin Scott, age 46. This your current address? How long have you lived there?"

"Twenty years," Martin sighed, in surprise, even in shame at being still in this nowhere, halfway between San Francisco and L.A. Neither city nor suburb, neither white nor integrated, neither rich nor poor, it wasn't even clearly defined. It had simply spread out like a spattered ink blot and filled up with people from all points east. Like this cop with his nasal accent: Iowa, probably. Maybe men like him liked living here. You couldn't tell. His face was too young to have acquired any set expression of his feelings, too young almost to be a face at all.

The other guy was muttering his answers; Martin didn't even hear his name. He had almost forgotten what he looked like. They hadn't looked at each other since the cop grabbed them and dragged them out into the park, slamming them up against the tree and patting them from shoulders to shins. "F-fifty-one," stammered the quivering voice. Martin glanced at him in disgust. He was trembling like an old woman, biting his lip, his face almost green. Still, he looked younger than fifty, one of those slight, fair, tight-skinned men who'd stay thin and unlined till he was sixty.

Martin's build was heavier, but between swimming and hiking he'd kept a flat belly and a firm jaw. When Marta was fourteen, her girlfriends had flirted with him and said things like, "Your dad's cute!" But he never really thought about his looks, not until lately, when Marta's friends from the university met him with a blank nod and pronounced, "Mr. Scott," with nothing but dead deference.

He shivered. Across the park lawn, on the sidewalk, the sun shone, but here under the trees the damp chill in the wet grass crept up his legs. He watched the people walking along the sunny sidewalk, slowing, turning to stare. Let them. He didn't care. They only made him feel tired, the way he always felt lately. Was it true that advancing age was felt mainly as fatigue? In men. Not women. Lynn had more energy now than when she was seventeen. She was always running off to a meeting or a class. No one could say that he had not encouraged his wife to go back to school, to join political groups, to do whatever she wanted.

"Okay, Scotty, into the car." The cop walked behind them toward the patrol car parked at the curb outside the park.

No one called him Scotty except Lynn. She'd asked him, when they met in that limp Alabama town she could not wait to get out of, if he wanted to be called Scotty. Definitely not. Scotty, he told her, sounded like an old dog crouched by the stove, scratching his fleas. Martin was his name. It meant warlike, a fighter, a warrior. Lynn compromised by calling him Marty, and she was the one who insisted the first baby be named after him.

Then, after Marta was born, Lynn had started calling him Scotty. It was too confusing, she said, calling them both Marty. And he decided it didn't matter. But now, all these years later, it suddenly hit him like a long-standing, unadmitted insult. It did matter. It did mean something.

He had trouble getting into the car. There were only inches of leg room in the back seat behind the metal grill that went from floor to ceiling. He turned his feet sideways to make them fit on the floor, and his knees pressed against the grill. The other guy huddled in the corner, his hands covering his face. The curious people came closer now, as if viewing fierce but safely caged animals. They stood still on the pavement and watched while the policeman fastened the seat belt over Martin's thighs, as if performing a loving service for an invalid. "Not too tight?" he asked. Martin's throat thickened and his eyes burned. Another chill ran through him, then a shudder of nausea. He was all right, he had stopped the tears. He'd learned how to stop the tears before he was twelve. But lately there came this chill and nausea when he blocked them, as if the tears turned acid and ran down his throat and through his body.

He leaned back but kept his head erect, his face forward. The car was sun-warmed, the motion soothing. He looked through the metal grill at the back of the cop's head. His brown hair curled at the top of his collar. His neck was smooth, baby skin. He must be very young. But everyone seemed young these days: school principals, opera stars, cops. It was depressing. "Male menopause," Lynn would croon, if he said it, the way she used to say, "Steve's fussy, needs his nap." Martin had gotten so that he could tell when it was coming, so he could swallow his irritation and turn on her with a huge smile.

The car pulled into a parking lot filled with official cars. The cop helped Martin out of the car, led him to a narrow metal door set in the blank back wall of a squat building, then opened the door and motioned Martin in ahead of him.

Martin faced a long, steep stairway. Ordinarily his wind was good, but he still felt nauseous, and his legs were still cold, dead. He had to haul them like great weights pulled forward from the hips, toes stumbling against the metal trim on the edge of each step. Finally, he grabbed the metal railing with his two manacled hands and hauled himself upward. He thought of the sprints he and Stephen made, racing each other up the stairs, ever since Steve was first able to walk, when Martin made a show of running up but always let little Steve win. Later the race was real, and they pushed and bumped dangerously against one another, laughing and gasping.

Last year, in one of his attempts to break through Steve's adolescent silence, Martin had challenged him at the foot of the school stairs, but Lynn turned to Steve and said, "Don't encourage him, he'll have a heart attack or something." Martin had laughed the loudest of them all. He never let himself be angry at Lynn, who at forty had begun to look younger, like a skinny boy, since she stopped wearing make-up, cut her hair, and adopted the blue jeans an cotton shirt uniform all these women wore.

At seventeen, with skinny hips and barely pricked out chest, she had seemed to worship him, the twenty-four-year-old college graduate who came and carried her off to California. Martin's father had told him he ought to be even older than his wife, at least ten years older, to clearly establish his authority, but even more because women aged, wore out, faster than men. No more. Nothing worked any more according to the rules the old man had lived by. Not that Martin ever thought they should. His father had been hopelessly patriarchal, like something left over from the last century, and Martin only quoted him as a joke.

Reaching the top of the stairway, Martin looked across a dark space. Partitions chopped off unseen places from which came metal rattles and muffled voices. In the middle of the space stretched a long table surrounded by chairs. In every chair sat a policeman in tan uniform, and as Martin stepped into the room, they all stood up. But none of them turned toward him. It was the end of a meeting, he realized, and they scattered without noticing him.

He was noticed by a policeman sitting at a desk near a window. The window looked into a brightly lit room no bigger than a closet. As Martin was steered toward the window, he saw that the inside of the windowed room was pink. It was the same color pink as the inside of the rest room in the park. The town must have bought a truckload of pink paint at a bargain price. Martin began to imagine pink police cars, pink garbage trucks. Probably the damned high school would get covered in pink next summer.

The cop got up from his desk. He was taller than Martin, black, and looked about forty. He had very red eyes and an unhealthy puffiness in his cheeks. He and the younger cop exchanged some words, but Martin did not begin to listen until it was too late to catch their sense. He was having trouble concentrating.

"In here."

Martin stepped inside the pink closet. On three sides, windows looked out into the gloomy inner room. A bright light in the ceiling was covered with thick glass laced with wire. A long bench stretched across the narrow space. There was hardly any room to stand.

The other guy had disappeared, probably taken to another pink closet. Martin felt relieved not to have to look at his panic-green face or listen to his shuddering breathing. It was disgusting to see a man let go of himself that way. Martin had shrunk away from him as from a man with a contagious disease.

"Shoes, coat, and belt."

"What?"

The cop was looking at him intently. He reached forward, unlocked the handcuffs, and took them off. "I have to take your shoes, coat, and belt."

"Oh. All right." Martin sat down on the bench and unlaced his boots. They were good hiking boots, just broken in, and he loved wearing them although the weather was a bit warm for heavy boots. Not warm enough for sandals yet. He handed the boots to the cop, then stood up to take off his belt and his coat, which was really a thick old sweater Lynn had knitted for him when she was pregnant. That was impossible for him to imagine anymore, Lynn pregnant and knitting.

"Stand up. Face the wall. Put your hands up on the wall. Higher. Spread your legs."

Martin leaned over the bench, his palms pushing against the pink wall while the policeman searched him again. He hadn't realized how tired he was until he had sat down to take off his boots. Now he longed to sit down again, to lie down if possible. How thoughtful the police were to have provided a bench so that a tired man could lie down.

"Okay. Now I'll take your driver's license over to the telecom center, where we run a check on you, for previous arrests, traffic citations, that kind of thing." The cop's manner had changed. He was actually polite. Martin took out his wallet and handed it over. The cop took out the driver's license, then handed the wallet back to him. "I'll be back in a few minutes, Mr. Scott. I'm Officer Sully. Mike Sully."

Martin wondered if he was expected to say, pleased to meet you, or to shake hands. He nodded and felt himself sinking down onto the bench.

"You okay? Want a drink of water or anything?"

Martin shook his head, and Officer Sully backed out, closing the windowed door behind him.

Martin sat, pressing his back against the cold pink wall as he looked through the thick windows in front of him and on both sides. The black policeman sat facing him, though never looking directly at him. All else was murky and grimy and dull outside his bright, private chamber. He felt more like a patient than a prisoner, maybe because they had taken his boots. It was like being in one of those examination rooms where you stripped and waited for the doctor.

He stretched out on his back, his feet hanging just slightly over the edge of the bench. But as soon as he closed his eyes, he felt the leaden chill in his legs spreading. His body was like a half-filled bottle turned on its side, its contents rushing upward through the neck to the cork. The full impact of what had happened to him surged up to choke him, and brought with it the worst fear of all, that he would not be a man. He might tremble or throw up or even cry, here, in front of these men or in front of Lynn when they called her. He imagined Lynn, standing outside in the gloomy room, looking in at him as she would look into one of the lighted fish tanks at the San Francisco aquarium.

He knew how to hold himself together: imagine something pleasant, a happy time, a time when he felt strong. What was a good age? Twenty-three, when he was meandering across the country on a motorcycle. No. He always told people those were the best two years of his life, those years between college and Alabama, where Lynn and marriage had suddenly grabbed him. But that was a lie. He'd been lonely and uncomfortable most of the time. The first few years after they were married were better. The babies were little miracles he'd made. And he didn't mind teaching, even enjoyed the way the teenagers were drawn to him because he was young, almost like them. He was comfortable at school and at home. Not fulfilled or even satisfied, but comfortable. An old scene came vividly to his mind: sitting in the rocking chair, reading, hearing sounds of Lynn bathing the kids, reading to them, then bringing them in to kiss him goodnight.

"How you doing?"

Martin had not heard Officer Sully come back in. He was not a bad guy really. He had intelligent brown eyes, not mean. Maybe he had been rough in the park because there were two of them, and Martin was big. He might have been afraid. But now he was relaxed, and he looked at Martin with a human face. He had a scrubby brown moustache and sideburns. He probably grew as much hair as regulations allowed, to show people he was a relaxed, humane man. One of the new breed of cops. A bit overeducated, a bit uncomfortable in his role.

"Want to talk while we wait for the telecom?"

Martin sat up and nodded. He moved over toward his left so that Officer Sully could sit on the bench beside him. Sully held a clipboard and a pen. The top sheet on the clipboard was covered with writing, probably Sully's report. Martin thought of asking to read it, then decided he didn't want to.

"Let's see, we got your age and address. Married?"

"Yes."

"Children?"

"A daughter, twenty-one, and a son, eighteen." Stephen. What would Stephen say? Would this pry open his mouth, make him talk to Martin, if only to curse him? Just the generation gap, Lynn said as if that explained anything. It was easier for her. A woman could cry and scream and throw things to arouse some response. Lynn could reach Steve, sometimes, because she had some contact, some real ties unbroken, ties formed during all those years of diapering and bathing and rocking and nursery school meetings and PTA, those Sundays in the park while Martin was off backpacking. Martin felt sure that had given her an advantage, though she denied it. It had been easier to let her do it, and easy to justify with another of his father's principles: menial child care was for women; they weren't bored as easily as a man. The father's role came later, when the child was older. Then the father set standards, and instilled reason, and. . . but Martin wasn't like his father, not that stiff, unapproachable statue he'd feared more than respected. A man couldn't be like that with his children today; he'd be laughable. But then, what could he be?

"Occupation?"

"Teacher."

Officer Sully looked at him with an expression so mixed that Martin could not read it. "Where do you teach?"

"Southeast High School."

Sully kept staring at the clipboard as if reading a long, absorbing story. "Well, I guess the telecom won't show any previous record, or you wouldn't be teaching." His silence then said that teaching was all over for Martin. Martin searched the young face for a vindictive look or for conviction that he was saving hundreds of students from depravity. What he saw was much worse: pity.

"I never really liked teaching," Martin said, almost defiantly. "I've been wanting to quit for a long time, but with a family to support. . . and when you're over forty, you can't just. . ." Sully was watching him. Martin knew he should stop talking. This soft manner of Sully's was probably only intended to make him admit things that he would later regret saying, though he didn't know why he'd regret saying he hated his job. He'd never meant to be a teacher. It was just something that popped up, and for a man with nothing but a college degree, it was something to do until. . . until what? "I guess I never really knew what I wanted to do. Did you always want to be a cop?"

Sully shook his head.

"It's funny," Martin went on, "I always assumed I was going to do something that would be interesting, important, but I never had any idea just what it would be. I just assumed. . . you know life is all assumptions. You think there's purpose and decision, but that's just an assumption too. . . like a man's assumption that he'll

...you know, do something." Sully was squinting and frowning as if he heard but could not understand. Of course, he couldn't, not at his age.

Suddenly Martin smiled, but managed to hold back his laughter. Another scene had flashed on in his mind, this time an imaginary one. Just a face, the face of his principal, with his busy little eyes and his pompous grin and his tight jaw, all loosening, sagging when he heard, his mind clouded with terror at what Martin's transgression might do to his own chances for superintendent. It would almost be worth it, to see his face.

Then Lynn's face intruded again, but he couldn't form the expression it would take when she learned that her means of support was gone. She might even have to get a job. Doing what? For all her college courses and conferences and workshops, she'd never held anything but that part-time waitress job in Alabama. She'd never known what it meant to go on day after day, year after year, as the gap between the students and you grew wider and wider, and they started to look at you the way the young look at the old. Martin knew the meaning of the look because he remembered exactly how he had felt about middle-aged people when he was young. They were done, finished, nonexistent. What a special torture teaching was. What could be more cruel than to subject a man to those looks from kids, day after day after...

"You had a checkup lately?"

"What?"

"Medical checkup. Like seeing a doctor?" Sully had put the clipboard down on his lap and had been watching Martin, for how long, Martin did not know. "I mean, I made an arrest on a charge like this a few months ago, only this was with the guy's patients, masturbating in front of them, all of a sudden, a man fifty-seven years old. Turned out he had a brain tumor. He was dead in three weeks."

Martin shook his head at Sully the way he used to do at Lynn in those early years when she hadn't even read a book. "There's nothing wrong with me. What's wrong are those stupid laws they pay you to enforce." It felt good to talk back to the young cop. To challenge, to argue a rational point, always made him feel clear-headed, in control. Push a personal question out into its social context, and it became clear, safer to handle, like nuclear material manipulated by metal talons behind a lead and glass shield.

Sully gave him a shifty, sullen look, and Martin knew he had him. He was too smart, this new kind of cop, not to know Martin was right.

"Yes, stupid charges, whatever they are...you haven't even told me what all those numbers mean, let alone...." Martin almost added his insistence on his right to make a phone call, but when he thought of calling anyone, the chill began to grab his legs again. He wasn't ready yet. He didn't even really want to hear the charges, but Sully was starting to recite, looking stiff and official again.

"647a, disorderly conduct: loitering in or about any toilet open to the public for the purpose of engaging in or soliciting any lewd or lascivious or any unlawful act. 288a, oral copulation, felony."

Martin hoped that the rising heat he felt was not a blush. The words seemed to echo around him in a courtroom full of women, the kind of woman who seemed to be in and out of the house at all hours these days. A few years ago, when Martin walked into a room full of Lynn's women friends, they smiled, crossed their legs, brightened as if the sun shone on them. Now, when he walked into a room full of women, he could never be sure what his reception might be. Sitting there, in his own house, they eyed him with a brief, measuring glance, then ignored him, or stared coolly. Last week he'd referred to them as Lynn's lesbian gang, laughing to cover his vague feeling of humiliation. Lynn didn't bother to deny it. Lately she didn't react at all when he teased her about her friends or her activities.

"Stupid!" he said, a little louder than he intended, but in a good, deep, controlled voice. "To legislate people's private lives."

"Public, man, public. People don't want to go into a public can and find you perverts..." Sully stopped and turned red as he stood up, shaken out of his cool pose, too shaken, Martin hoped, to see how the word *perverts* had stung Martin.

"It's the law that's perverted, persecuting people who..."

"And you're okay." Sully sneered like a sullen kid.

Martin shrugged, a good, smooth shrug, with no sign of shaking. "I don't have your hangups about sex."

"Oh, yeah, and you're just like any all-American boy who does this all the time?"

Martin almost answered, but stopped. This was one of those trick questions, to get him to admit something. Though actually there was nothing to admit. This had been the first time, the only time.

Sully was shaking his head. "I'll never in a million years be able to understand you guys, *why* you pick that can, knowing how heavily we patrol it, forcing us to..."

Now Martin felt he must say something, must give some answer to oppose to this man's disgust, to hold off the contempt and pity raining down on him from Sully, pouring over him like filth. But what could he answer? He could not remember why he had gone to the park, could not remember planning to go there or even thinking about it. It had been an impulse, an accident. Its meaning eluded him, like the meaning of incongruous shapes in a dream.

Finally, unable to bear the look on Sully's half-turned face, he made himself shrug again, summoned a final surge of desperate bravado, and smiled. "I just wasn't getting enough at home, so this was the simplest and cheapest..." He was stopped by the look of stunned incredulity on Sully's face as the cop unlocked the door and let himself out.

Martin leaned forward, elbows on knees, keeping his head bowed to dispel the dizziness he'd felt when Sully looked at him that way. He was probably only hungry. It must be past dinner time. Lynn would worry. No, that was another scene from the past. Nowadays, mealtimes were casual, irregular stops when by chance they happened to meet for a few minutes, for a report, like the latest news, on what they were doing.

On what Lynn was doing. She didn't really listen to him, not the way she used to. Not the way they all used to. All his life he'd talked to women. Men couldn't talk to men, except about sports or cars or politics. But not about anything that mattered. Young, pretty women would fix their eyes on his and listen and nod when he told them what he could do, would do, what he thought and hoped. Until all that changed too, and they didn't listen anymore. Their eyes narrowed and they cut him off. They were bored. He'd asked Lynn, just last night, if women were becoming bored with men. He shouldn't have left himself open that way because she came right in on him with, "They were always bored, dear, but they used to pretend." It had taken all his control to make himself laugh, to hide his anger and to hide that feeling of being tripped, pushed off balance. He'd had that feeling so often lately, that rocky feeling, as if dozens of tiny, invisible supports had suddenly been pulled out from under him. But the doctor had said nothing was wrong, he was in great shape. For a man his age.

"Telecom check is clear. Not even a parking ticket."

Martin raised his head to see Sully holding out his driver's license to him. Martin took the license and put it back into his wallet. "Now what happens?"

"Fingerprints, photo."

"Then I can go?"

"Soon as you make bail. Five hundred dollars." He look apologetic about that, almost friendly again. "You can make a phone call anytime now."

Martin nodded. "Then what happens?"

Sully shrugged. "That's it."

"No, I mean. . .afterward." If he knew exactly what was going to happen, he could face it. When he was a boy, he had fantasies of terrible tests of his manhood in battles with monsters or in war. Later, in his teens, the tests of his courage were imagined as scenes of torture or execution. He had imagined himself, in a dozen different ways, facing death, with coolness, with courage. None of these tests had ever come. But now, what was happening now, would be that kind of test: a public execution of his reputation, his job, probably his marriage. Everything. It really was an annihilation, a death. And strangely, his fear of this death was mixed with something like relief, something like exhilaration. In any case, it would be a test, the test. And it seemed to him that if there were no surprises, if he knew at every step exactly what was coming, he would be able to face it all bravely, and behave well.

"Well, there's the arraignment in a couple of days."

"In court? Public?"

"That's right. They usually do arraignments in the late morning, right after traffic court."

"They read the charge out loud?"

Sully was shaking his head. "Don't worry, the judge just reads the numbers and the clerk hands you the charge in writing. It's all pretty quiet. Sometimes, sitting in the back, I couldn't even tell what was going on."

"You'll be there."

Sully shook his head again. "You won't see me again."

"Until the trial?"

Sully shrugged. "You're not going to trial."

"Not going. . ." Martin felt another test being taken away from him. "I have a right to a trial."

"Sure, sure, but that's not what's going to happen. You wanted to know what's going to happen."

Martin nodded and waited.

"At the arraignment the prosecutor will offer to drop all charges if you plead guilty to Disturbing the Peace, and waive trial. You get off with a fifty-dollar fine and probation. If you plead innocent and go to trial, I testify, and you get up to six months just on the 647d. Then there's the felony 288a. See? Everyone cops a plea. It's a lot easier on the family. And judges don't like to try these things. They figure you're hurt enough, your job and all, without going to jail. Once burned, twice careful. Don't get many repeaters."

"And that's all?" Martin fought against the cold weariness creeping up his legs again. "They just read off a number and I plead guilty to something else, and it's all over?"

Sully nodded. "Usually in less than five minutes. You want to make that phone call now?"

Yes, the phone call. That was something. There was still the phone call to Lynn. He stood up, quite erect. "I'd like to have my boots."

Sully nodded, opened the door, and pointed to Martin's boots and belt lying on the desk where the black officer still sat. Martin buckled his belt and stepped into his boots, bending easily to lace them. "Okay," he said firmly as he straightened. Sully led him across the gloomy space and behind a partition, where a phone sat on a long counter.

As Martin dialed, he sorted through the possible ways of telling Lynn. Perhaps he should tell her to sit down before he told her. No, she'd think something had happened to one of the kids. He might start by saying he'd had a slight accident. No, that would sound silly, apologetic. He wouldn't lie just to soften the blow. He'd just come straight out and say...no, that was too crude, harsh, not his style at all. No, the less said on the phone the better. He would just tell her to come and bring the money.

Then, when they were face to face, he'd tell her, quietly, with a shrug, if not a smile. He tried to imagine how she would react. She couldn't smile and ignore him this time. This would be an earthquake. His disgrace would spill over onto her. And the pity too, which, he had just learned, felt worse than disgrace. And the one use he still was to her, the money, would be taken from her. She would be forced to pay attention. She would be one woman who would start listening again. And she wouldn't be bored.

It was some time before he realized how long the phone had been ringing. It rang and rang. There was no one at home.

The Prig from Pleasant Hill

Actually, I was the one who called myself a prig. Leo used to laugh and say my use of such an old-fashioned word almost proved my point. My therapist asked what I meant exactly, and I tried to list the things that add up to being a prig, a conservative person who has never seen or done much, a not very interesting person. Living in Pleasant Hill for one thing, not as a trapped suburban housewife but at home with my parents, just because I grew up there and had started teaching there. Being a graduate of Hayward State instead of Cal-Berkeley. Then a lot of little things, like wearing glasses, being on time, and writing a round, clear, schoolteacher's penmanship. Have you ever known a really interesting person with legible handwriting? And, while I wasn't a virgin, there'd only been Walter, and I'd thought I was going to marry him. So, in desperation, on my twenty-third birthday I got fitted with contact lenses and moved into an apartment in Berkeley.

I met Leo the first week, at a lecture called Unleashing Your Potential, at the Unitarian Church. I was standing in the atrium by the fountain, wondering whether to go out and pretend to look at the view or just give up and go back to my apartment. Leo came up to me and said that if I'd let down my hair, I'd look just like Aleta in the Prince Valiant comic strip.

I don't remember now what I thought he looked like, whether I thought he was handsome or not. Medium height, medium build, somewhere in his forties, with a kind voice and dreamy eyes, not dull or distant, but slow-reacting. Now that I see him so differently, it's hard to remember what attracted me. My therapist and I discussed all the usual possibilities: my loneliness, inadequacy, need of a father figure and so on. But, as I finally told her, everyone knows older men are nicer than young men and more interesting; they know more and have done more. They're proud of having a young blonde to take around. And usually they're calm and easy because they have a mature wife who is taking care of the petty details of life.

Leo told me he was separated from his wife. Later on I found out that when I met him he was still living with her and his son in one of those housing tracts in Pinole, where they'd lived for twenty years. But I don't hold that against him because within the week they really had separated.

Two weeks after we met, he called and asked if I wanted to go with him to an unblocking seminar. I hesitated but didn't want to show how ignorant I was by asking what it was.

". . . and necessary for my research."

"What research?"

"I'll explain later."

The unblocking seminar met in the basement of an old house on Grove Street, where traffic noise almost drowned out the sound of the six-foot gong which the group leader struck while we all lay on the floor and vibrated.

On the way home Leo explained. He was an optometrist with an office in the La Marina Shopping Plaza. During the past couple of years he had become interested in the old sight-without-glasses movement, studying Bates and Corbett and Aldous Huxley. He had become convinced that wearing glasses was unnecessary and that the key to perfect vision was relaxation. Bates had failed to catch on, he said, because he didn't go far enough. Leo was developing a total body-mind relaxation treatment which would draw on eastern spiritual disciplines, massage, hypnotism, psychological and physical awareness techniques, in fact, on all the "growth therapies." When he was ready, he would start a treatment center which combined the best of old and new knowledge to give people perfect sight without glasses. In the meantime, to support his wife and son, he was still fitting glasses at the shopping center. It was his wife's resistance to new ideas that had finally broken them up. She was strictly middle-age suburban, he said, completely inflexible. "Curiously," he said, with a soft laugh and a shrug, "she still has twenty-twenty vision."

We went to bed almost as soon as we got into my apartment. I made some feeble protest, which he called my Pleasant Hill mentality, and that's how the joke started. The next day he moved in, and the day after that he made me stop wearing my contact lenses.

I didn't really mind giving them up because they felt so uncomfortable slithering around on my eye balls, sometimes catching a beam of light or speck of dust that stabbed like a sword driven through my skull. I kept a pair of glasses in my car for the commute to Pleasant Hill, but the rest of the time I lived in a blurred world without having any serious problems except that I tired easily.

"You see," said Leo, "we've already given you more confidence. That's the beginning of the end of tension."

When we weren't making love, he was working on me, trying every new relaxation technique. I learned yoga, six meditation systems, massage, self-hypnosis, est, and neo-primal screaming, which I had to quit because it made me too hoarse to teach. I spent a half hour four times a day doing eye exercises. I alternately sunned and palmed my eyes whenever I was resting. But I was a disappointing subject for Leo's research. During the whole time I walked around half-seeing the world, I made no progress, no matter what Leo tried. He used to sigh and say there must be some deep, unconscious resistance in me. I told him I wouldn't be a bit surprised and promised to try my best to overcome it.

Some of the growth groups we went to ended up with everyone nude, and at first I was pretty shy about that. Then I discovered that groups of naked people are very polite and formal, always looking each other in the eyes, and never slouching. But just about the time I lost my self-consciousness, Leo decided nude counseling was superficial.

We read a lot of books on sex techniques and tried them all because orgasm, Leo said, was total relaxation. I did awfully well, having one orgasm after another, though my vision didn't improve. Then one night, after a hard day at school, I said I was tired and wanted to sleep, and suddenly Leo started yelling. At first I thought he was kidding, but he wasn't. He raved about how his ex-wife (the divorce had gone through by then) always said she was tired and kept him frustrated for twenty years, and on and on. After that I never told him when I didn't feel like it, and if I didn't have an orgasm, I'd pretend to.

I was happiest, I think, when we had his boy with us. Jerry was thirteen years old, with freckles and curly red hair and the sweetest crooked smile you ever saw. I was afraid that he would hate me—the younger woman who took his father away. So I did everything I could think of to keep that smile on his face during the weekends he spent with us. And when Jerry told his mother he wanted to come live with us, and she agreed, I was in heaven. My therapist said that's because I was trying to prove to myself that I was lovable. Maybe, I told her, but I also just like kids, and they usually like me.

So we got married, and Jerry came to live with us, and we bought a house, using my savings as a down payment. It was a real old-Berkeley house, the kind everyone who comes to Berkeley wants: two stories, with brown shingles on the outside and a fireplace and lots of dark woodwork inside. I filled it with funny old furniture and rugs, and pinned posters on the walls. There were some drawbacks. It was a little drafty and leaky and too near the campus, surrounded by students who played loud music day and night. But I was the only one who minded. Leo liked being around young people.

A little while after we moved in, he took up weaving. When I think of him now, I always see him at his loom. He had put it in the dining alcove in front of a huge mirror which almost covered the wall. He sat facing the mirror, usually with a cigarette hanging from his lips, and from across the room I could look up from a book or some schoolwork and see him in the mirror, guiding the shuttle back and forth. He had grown a moustache which came in black and silky, curling down around his mouth so that when he narrowed his eyes against the cigarette smoke, he looked exotic and inscrutable.

There was a little room in the back of the house that Leo used for his vision work. He put in an examination chair, a green plush couch, and a record player. He hung seven mobiles from the ceiling and covered the walls with charts: eye, astrological, acupuncture and kundalini yoga. In this room he saw patients who wanted to get rid of their glasses. He thought he might be in for trouble with the optometrical association if he saw them at his office, so he kept this work quite separate. He went to his office in the morning. In the afternoons he saw people, mostly young people, at home in his vision room for sight-without-glasses training.

One of them was Nancy, a sixteen-year-old girl who always stopped to talk to me when she was through seeing Leo. I was wearing my hair loose by then, and she used to ask me if she could brush it because I looked just the way she imagined the princesses in the fairy tales. Nancy had been doing eye exercises with Leo since he first started them, when she was only thirteen, and had managed to avoid wearing glasses at all. She was small and dark: Filipino, Indian and Irish. She was so delicate, with her hair cut short like a cap, and she moved like a mischievous, dancing elf. She said I was the princess held in thrall by a wily sorcerer and bade do impossible tasks, and she was Rumpelstiltskin, who could do everything for me by magic. She made me laugh, yet like an elf in a fairy tale, she seemed wise and old. Kids raised in Berkeley are like that sometimes.

When I said to my therapist that the first month in the house was perfect, she raised her eyebrows and asked if there weren't doubts even then. For instance, money. I never had any idea how much money Leo made, only that he was always broke and getting phone calls from bill collectors or letters from his ex-wife's lawyer. He'd laugh and shrug and say he'd always been rotten with money, and I'd better keep my money separate or I'd always be worrying, making tensions that would hold back progress with my eyes. So I did, but ended up paying all the household bills so there wasn't much left to keep separate.

And then there was Jerry, who started getting moody soon after he moved in, closing up and looking secretive, as if he was up to something. Leo didn't notice anything, and when I talked about it, he said that Jerry had always been a very difficult kid, and that's why his mother had been willing to let him go. The first time we learned Jerry was cutting school and I got upset, Jerry said I wasn't his mother and couldn't tell him what to do, and Leo just looked sad and said the schools were awful anyway. Nancy said being a teenager was tough and she would talk to him, but he just gave her a terrible look which I didn't understand until much later.

Meanwhile, Leo had found a new group that met in a house in the Oakland hills with a pool and a Japanese hot tub. After swimming, soaking and massage, the group leader gave a lecture on the therapeutic value of communal, nonpossessive sex in a protected environment. When she started demonstrating with Leo and another man, I went out and crouched in the hot tub until Leo came to me. He put his arms around me and kissed me and told me he loved me and that was the only reason he was doing all this. "Your resistance just proves how much she can teach us. And I doubt you're going to experience clear vision until you can free yourself of jealousy."

So I promised to try, and I did. I started participating just like everyone else, and I was proud of myself when I managed to have orgasms as good as any I used to have with Leo. But then Leo suddenly insisted we drop out, saying we'd gotten all we could out of it.

He started going out alone a couple of nights a week. He said he had to explore some groups which didn't allow couples. Sometimes he was out until two or three in the morning. Usually I'd lie awake waiting for him, but by the time he came, I'd be so upset that I'd pretend to be asleep. Jerry started going out on those nights too and staying out almost as late as Leo. The night the police called to say they'd picked Jerry up in a stolen car, Leo wasn't home, so I left a note and went down to the police station, where I waited until he came to pick us both up at three a.m.

That night I lost my temper. I guess I was tired from working all day and not sleeping. I screamed and yelled, and when Leo tried to make me relax, I screamed all the more. He looked crushed. He cried and told me he loved me and wanted nothing but good for me. It would kill him, he said, to fail me, to fail this second marriage. He suggested we go to a marriage counselor and see if we couldn't work out our problems.

The first one we went to listened to us for an hour, then said he thought we had irreconcilably opposed attitudes toward marriage and that what we really wanted was a divorce. Leo laughed all the way home, saying how impossibly square the man was. I laughed too; the thought of divorce seemed so absurd, unthinkable. We decided we could work things out better by ourselves, so I started reading books on open marriage and had to admit they were very logical and rational.

Leo kept searching for the missing factor that would clear my sight. He thought I might make a quicker breakthrough if we tried some drugs. He had already introduced me to pot (how he laughed when I confessed I'd never tried it, though it was just as plentiful in Pleasant Hill as anywhere in Berkeley), and now he started bringing home other things. Except for one very bad series of hallucinations, the things he tried on me had no effect, except to make me nervous whenever I saw him coming at me with a new one. So he gave up, sighing and saying that my lack of trust would wipe out any benefits.

On the nights he went out alone, Nancy started coming to stay with me. She had turned seventeen and had already left school and rented a room near our house. We did our eye exercises together and talked and listened to music. Our friendship was cemented the night that Jerry called the police and turned us in for possession of marijuana. The police came, but as soon as they saw we weren't drug dealers, they laughed, made jokes about teenage pranks (Jerry was out, of course, by the time they came), and left. Nancy and I laughed, but then I started shaking and couldn't stop. I kept shaking and shaking while Nancy held me in her arms and rocked me and kissed me. Finally she crawled into bed with me and held me till I fell asleep. When I woke up, she was gone, Leo was beside me, and it was past time to get up. I drove so fast I almost had an accident on the way to Pleasant Hill that morning. And later the principal called me in. He was worried about the way I looked and said some of the reports I'd turned in were illegible. I made some excuse, I can't remember what.

Leo was out almost every night now, and when he came home he usually woke me up to talk, to tell me if he'd been with any women. He said that proved we had a special, free relationship few people could achieve. He'd kiss me and tell me how much he loved me, then turn over and go to sleep. Then I would lie awake, wondering if I could ever live up to this ideal relationship.

Meanwhile, to work out Jerry's problems, Leo had found another family counselor, and the three of us went every week for a while. Jerry just sat there and refused to talk. And I couldn't bring up certain questions about Leo and me in front of Jerry. So Leo did most of the talking, comparing notes with the counselor on different growth therapies. The counselor was in a Jungian dance group and wanted us to go, but I was too tired, so Leo went alone. He never seemed to be tired. When I got home from school I'd find him weaving. He'd already been to his office and had given a few home eye-training sessions. A short nap and a quick dinner, and he was ready to go out again.

I finally started confiding in Nancy, crying a lot and pouring out my mixed up feelings. She never said anything, just hugged me and kissed me and cuddled with me in bed a lot. Then I started to kiss her too, and she said we loved each other. I really got confused then, and frightened that I was seducing this young girl because of tendencies I didn't even know I had until then. Finally, I told Leo about Nancy and me, but all he said was that I must be free, and my freedom would eventually lead to total relaxation and clear sight.

A few days later, I felt sick at school. I left early and came home to find Leo and Nancy in our bed. I think nothing Leo had done hurt me so much. I accused him of stealing my friend. But he and Nancy smiled at each other, then at me, and told me they had been lovers since she was fourteen. I started vomiting, and Leo said he would find us another marriage counselor.

This time I told all my true feelings, even if they were priggish and old-fashioned. And Leo said he would do anything to save our marriage. First of all, Nancy was out, for good. And Leo wasn't interested in going to any more growth groups; he thought he'd exhausted whatever they could offer to his vision work. He still wanted to go to the dance class, but would be home by eleven. We talked about his age and his need for female admiration, and the counselor suggested it would be easier for us to work things out if I saw Leo's behavior as a symptom of male menopause. Leo sighed and nodded and said he'd soon be forty-five, and if he lost me, he'd kill himself.

About the time we finished with that counselor, Jerry was picked up in the process of a burglary. When the police saw how upset we were, they were very nice, gave us a list of things stolen throughout the past few months, and asked us to search our house. In the attic and the backs of closets we found three tape recorders, two record players, six transistor radios, two guitars and seventeen watches. Leo cried, held Jerry in his arms and said we hadn't given him enough love and that Jerry was stealing love. Jerry didn't answer. I hadn't heard the sound of his voice for weeks, except to ask me for money. Leo never seemed to have any to give him.

During this time we forgot our own difficulties, even forgot the decisions we'd made, so that somehow we drifted back to the old ways, with Leo out late three or four nights a week. And one of those nights Nancy showed up. I was feeling so alone, I was glad to see her. I'd missed her. Leo got home early that night, and the three of us went to bed together. He and Nancy said they were sorry they had kept their relationship from me, but they hadn't known how to tell me, knowing I was so priggish about things like that. From now on we would all love one another, and everything would be open between us.

Leo and Nancy still wanted to have some time alone, but not behind my back. So they would tell me when they wanted the house to themselves, and I would go out and walk, and walk. On the nights Leo went out alone, Nancy took me out to some places I don't think even Leo had been to. She told Leo she thought I didn't have any inhibitions left, and Leo said he thought he was noticing some improvement in my eyes, though everything seemed as blurred as ever to me. But I was used to a blurred world and even preferred it to the sharp, defined edges that I saw when I put on my glasses to drive.

Then I got sick. It started with a pain during intercourse with Leo, and suddenly became a cramp so bad that I fainted. When I came to, the pain was still there, so bad I couldn't stand. The doctor couldn't find anything wrong, but after a few days he decided to do an exploratory D and C, in case there was some undetected uterine infection or tumor.

I came out of the anesthetic crying. The doctor said everything was fine, no tumor, no sign of disease. But I couldn't seem to get out of bed, and when my parents came to see me, I started crying again. They asked me if I wanted to come home with them for a few days to recuperate. So I let them take me.

Leo called me every day to ask when I was coming home. Nancy called too, giggling and calling herself Rumpelstiltskin and saying she missed me. I couldn't eat, and I got weaker and weaker. Leo said he'd get in touch with our last counselor, but I said no. Then my father called our old family doctor, and he recommended a therapist.

My father drove me to her every day for a month, and I cried through every session. Then I cried when Leo called me each night. Especially when he told me that Nancy had moved into the house with him. The vision of him at his loom and Nancy standing behind him, the two of them reflected in that huge mirror, haunted me, gave me nightmares. But my therapist said she was sure it wouldn't last long. "Not without you there," she said with an ironic smile.

She was right. Leo called me only a week later to tell me Nancy had walked out, saying she would leave Berkeley because it was getting to be full of suburban freak-outs. Then Leo's ex-wife called and said Leo had tried to get her to take him back, but she wouldn't. She just wanted me to know that she was taking Jerry back and that she didn't blame me for anything Jerry had done. She added that Leo had been beaten and his office smashed up by the father of one of his patients. "I guess I don't have to tell you why." Then Nancy called and said that Leo had been impotent ever since I left. She had decided to stay in Berkeley, had moved into the YWCA and enrolled at Laney College to study computer programming. Then Leo called again to ask for money to make the next payment on the house. He told me his forty-fifth birthday was coming on Saturday, and he wanted to celebrate it with me. When he started crying, I hung up and told my father to get me a lawyer.

I thought the worst was over then, but I was wrong. The worst was the way I hated myself for getting into such a mess and taking over a year to get out of it. Maybe I was just what Nancy said, a suburban freak-out who played crazy in Berkeley for a while before going back home to settle down. Worse than a prig, a hypocrite! I called myself a lot of other names before my therapist finally took my hand and said, "Look, sometimes our best qualities get twisted around and used against us." I didn't know what she meant, but she made me feel better. "I don't think you'll make the same mistakes again," she said.

"No, I'll make new ones."

She nodded, and we laughed.

And I put on my glasses and went back to work.

I guess my parents hoped that I would stay in Pleasant Hill. "You're not going back to Berkeley!" my mother said.

"Don't blame Berkeley," I said. "Leo was from Pinole." Then I tried to explain to my parents that I had to leave home and try again.

"Try what?"

"I don't know," I told them. "All I know is that I'm still hoping to find or to be something different."

"That's only what everyone hopes for," sighs my father, "even in Pleasant Hill."

Catherine's Room

"Is there anyone whose name I didn't call?"

A pale girl in the back row raised her hand, leaning forward with eyes and mouth widening. Her blonde head swayed on her long neck as if she were trying to glimpse something behind Catherine.

"Did you register for the class?"

The girl shook her head. "I was hoping..." Her high, breathy voice thinned to a sigh.

Catherine looked around the room. "You see we're full. Sorry."

The girl only sank back in her chair and kept her eyes on Catherine.

Catherine began with some new readings she had selected from Emily Dickinson, George Orwell and I. B. Singer, trying to ignore the restless shuffling which began as soon as she did. For twelve years she had faced remedial writing classes full of hostile, anxious eighteen-year-olds at Bay Junior College. She did not find her students contemptible, as most of her colleagues did. She did not wish she were teaching at the University of California, as they did. She read all papers conscientiously and was the only instructor in the English department who allowed unlimited rewrites. Yet she reached few students. The sullen resistance and the high drop-out rate mystified and discouraged her. Lately she had begun to wonder if what frightened students away was the possibility of change. Familiar pain and failure were more comfortable than the challenge she offered. But she could not offer anything less.

107

"Are there any questions?"

Several students turned to look at the clock. Catherine dismissed the class, picked up her things, and headed downstairs. She shared an office with two new teachers who had settled in with plants, posters, coffee cups, and piles of books. One kept an FM radio tuned to a station which played baroque music all day. Catherine had begun to feel like an intruder. It was not that they crowded her out, but rather that she had never felt so at home here, so settled, as they instantly were.

The office was empty. She left the door wide open, as usual, inviting students who seldom came for help. As she sat down, she heard a sound, a rustling, breathy movement. It was the girl with the long neck, her tall, narrow body swaying slightly as she leaned on the door jamb.

"Could I talk to you, please?" she begged, in a breathy gush.

Catherine motioned her to a chair.

"After I heard you tell about your rewriting policy, I knew I just had to have your class. Really, I haven't got a snitch of self-confidence because I've been out of school since high school, twelve years! I'm so ignorant, I just..."

"Twelve years? You're thirty years old?"

The blonde head wiggled on its long stalk, and the smooth little mouth made a crooked grin. "Oh, yes, I'm older than I look. I guess I look young because I'm shallow. Ignorant. I don't know a thing! Or maybe because I don't have kids, so I'm still a kid. Michael and I have been married ten years, and nothing but two miscarriages. Doctors don't know what's wrong. Michael says I'm too nervous to get pregnant." The swaying, wiggling motions shifted from one part of her body to another as she unself-consciously jumped from one intimate detail of her life to another. "Look, I just have to be in your class because you're so...you're just such a neat woman!"

Catherine suppressed a smile as she silently agreed she could be called neat: short and compact, with sharp contrast between her clear golden skin, short black hair, and green eyes. She was forty, looked her age, and acted it. She knew that women admired her without envy because they saw how men were put off by her firm, searching gaze.

"What is your name?"

"Sally Gray." As she saw Catherine adding the name to the class list, she gave a squeal that she strangled into a gasp. "Oh, thank you so much!"

Catherine shrugged. "In a few weeks there'll be plenty of space."
She had not meant to say that aloud.

During those few weeks, as half the class drifted away, Sally
Gray attended every class with wide eyes in her constantly swaying
face. She smiled expectantly when Catherine entered the room.
She frowned fiercely when Catherine threw out a question for discussion. Often, when Catherine was talking, Sally gripped the edge
of the writing arm of her desk, swaying with excitement, glancing
around at the other students as if for confirmation that Catherine's
point was a brilliant insight. Sometimes she sank back in her chair
with a sigh, overcome by the total rightness of a concluding phrase.
When she spoke in her gaspy tremolo, she showed not only her
ignorance but a kind of wispy curiosity. She laughed at her mistakes
or pounded her head with a tight fist, her mouth wide, releasing a
breathy "ahhh!" of satisfaction when Cathering contradicted her.

Her gasps and wiggles might have been distracting to a brighter
class, but here they energized, stimulated the apathetic, even stimulated Catherine. The first time Sally was absent the class turned into
a dead weight, pulling Catherine down. It was no harder than her
other remedial writing classes, but until then Catherine had not
realized how much she had been energized by Sally's presence.

That afternoon Sally appeared in the open doorway of Catherine's
office. She was wearing a long skirt that clung to her narrowly fragile hips. Her neck looked longer than ever, as if she had suddenly
lost weight. Her head drooped sideways, as if her thin neck could
hardly hold it up. And her pale face seemed pulled downward into
long lines; she looked thirty.

"You're ill."

Sally sighed. "Migraine. It's all over now, I just look dead for a
while." She lowered herself carefully into the chair Catherine kept
beside her desk. "It hit me last night. Takes about eight hours.
Nothing helps. I've tried every kind of pill but..." she smiled,
gradually reviving as she talked. "Oh, and I had to miss your class!"

"We missed you!" said Catherine.

"Dumb me," Sally murmured, laughing with some effort. She
always laughed at Catherine's jokes.

"I'm serious," said Catherine. "The class was dead without you.
I think I ought to put in for a budget allotment marked Sally Gray
and have you paid just to sit in on all my classes."

"Well, you're such a neat teacher, I don't see how they can just sit there! Uh, listen, I'd like to. . . well, is it just too gauche of me? but do you ever accept invitations from students. . . I mean, would you come and have dinner with Michael and me?"

"I'd like to."

Sally let out a happy squeal. "Do you have a husband or a boyfriend you want to bring?"

Catherine shook her head.

"Oh, good! Then I won't have to be polite and pay attention to some old man when I really want to talk to you. And Michael won't bother us. I'll tell him to be quiet!" When she saw Catherine smile, she reached out and touched her arm, giving a slight, mischievous wiggle. "Friday night?"

Cathine nodded. "Where do you live?" She picked up a pencil.

"In Berkeley. On Shasta Road."

"Then you must be near me."

"Really!"

As Sally gave the house number, Catherine nodded. "Just a few blocks up. I could even walk it."

On Friday night she climbed the winding road up to the brown-shingled stack of attached boxes clinging to the side of the hill, hardly seen from the road, facing westward across flatlands and bay. It was just the sort of house Catherine's friends had been urging her to buy. She agreed with them, but kept putting off the trouble of looking, buying, moving.

"Oh, it's not ours!" gasped Sally, as she brought Catherine across the front room to see the view. "It belongs to a Cal professor who's on sabbatical, and we're just house-sitting. Next June we'll have to move out and find something else." She served a delicately herbed chicken on pale blue china plates set on the low coffee table. They sat on the floor, on pillows. "There's stacks of linens and everything, but I'd just have to wash it all. And this is nicer, by the window, don't you think?"

Michael was a dark, muscular little man whose thinning black hair lay in long fine lines across his wrinkled forehead. The wrinkles extended downward, all around his eyes, which squinted narrowly as if he were always looking into the sun. He looked his age, perhaps older, as if he and Catherine were contemporaries, enjoying the playful chatter of the child Sally.

Sally poked and teased Michael as she told Catherine about him and herself. She had grown up in a small town near Tahoe, where her father was a schoolteacher. At twenty she had met Michael on the ski slopes and married him. Since then they had worked in vacation resorts, then drifted until they ran out of money, then worked again for a while. A year ago Sally had insisted that they come to Berkeley, where Michael could go to the university and learn to become "...well, something besides a middle-aged lifeguard." They lived on student loans, in other people's houses, and on occasional part-time work Sally did, mostly housework. "But then I thought, why shouldn't I go to school too? Even if I am shallow? Something to do while Michael figures what he's going to be when he grows up." Michael squinted and smiled and said nothing.

While chattering about herself, Sally threw questions at Catherine, who answered them, telling more about herself than she ordinarily would. Sally's open chatter and the wine relaxed her, and she confessed some of her feelings of displacement and discouragement in her job.

"I know, I know!" Without looking at Michael, Sally said, "You should see how they just sit there. You're so brilliant...well, they're stunned, I'm stunned!"

"You mean I teach over their heads?"

"No, no, you're not over my head and that's pretty low! It's that you...you treat every one of us as if we can really think!"

"How else could I treat you?"

"You ought to be at the university!"

Catherine shook her head. "I'm not a scholar."

"Well, but you're not a bone-head English comma-chaser either! Just what are you!"

Catherine laughed, then surprised herself by admitting that she had once thought she was a poet. She even recited the sonnet that had been printed in an anthology of best poems five years ago.

"What are you writing now?"

Catherine shook her head. "I don't write anymore."

She stayed until midnight. Sally hugged her at the door, calling her Catherine. Then she goosed Michael, frowned, and groaned, "Time to fuck. Doctor's orders. My fertile time." The remark should have seemed pointlessly offensive, but popping out of Sally, it produced a tickling shock, a release of laughter which hurt no one. "Oh, I get away with a lot," Sally hooted. "Poor Michael!"

Catherine was still smiling at one of Sally's jokes when she got home. She walked down the dirt path on the side of the house and let herself into her apartment. It was really only one large room built into the basement of a downslope house like the one Sally and Michael lived in. Two of the three large storage closets behind the room had been converted into a tiny kitchen and bath. The only heat came from a huge stone fireplace in one corner. Catherine slept on a sofa-bed near the fireplace. On three walls she had built and filled bookshelves.

The fourth wall, facing the downhill garden, was made of one foot panes of glass set in rough wood frames, opening the room to the western sky. Catherine had set her desk in front of the broad wall of glass, where she could sit to work or just to look down into the sloping hillside garden.

When she moved in, nearly seven years before, she had looked out on a ragged tangle of overgrown brush and trees. The first year she had pruned the trees and bushes and dug out the weeds. Then year by year she planted, adding flowering plants near the window where the sun came strong. Further down she planted ferns and tropical plants under the trees. She rimmed the bottom property line and the sides of the house with star jasmine. Last year she had cut paths zigzagging among the trees and had begun hanging baskets of fuchsias from their branches. The old woman who owned the house and lived alone upstairs was apologetic about the cramped kitchen, the sluggish plumbing, the lack of heat, and delighted with the work Catherine did in the garden. She kept the rent low and promised that until she died no one would evict Catherine.

But Catherine's friends thought she should buy a house of her own, for comfort, for investment. Catherine was beginning to agree with them. The room had been perfect for her when she was spending her summers in Europe and most weekends out of town. But she no longer felt refreshed by unfamiliar places, just as she no longer wrote the verses that used to be printed in literary magazines.

Saturday morning the phone range at eight. "Oh, I hope I didn't wake you!" Sally's voice was even breathier on the phone, like a rush of wind. "I just finally got Michael pushed into a corner to make him study! And I was thinking...well, I know you've got a million other things to do and friends you can really talk to, but I mean...look, I feel like a walk up over in Tilden Park, and I just wondered if you..."

"Why, yes, I need a good hike."

At the top of the hill, rimming Berkeley and other towns north and south, lies a broad belt of regional parkland with lakes, grazing land, reservoirs: acres of open land with winding miles of paths. Sally and Catherine hiked on a ridge where they could see the towns and the bay on one side and the valley of reservoirs and grazing land on the other. Sally asked Catherine's opinion of Dickens, the present administration in Washington, Korean food, women's rights, and Bach. At noon they came back to Catherine's room, ate oranges and drank tea, propping up their tired feet while Sally admired the room and the garden. "Oh, I had such fun!" gushed Sally. "I'd just love to do this every Saturday."

And although ordinarily Catherine could not stand a gusher, she said sincerely, "So would I."

Throughout the fall and winter, except on a couple of rainy weekends, Catherine and Sally walked on Saturday morning. Catherine talked about poetry. Sally talked about herself and about Michael. When she mentioned him, her eyes lost some of their shine, and her wriggling motions became sharper, impatient. "If we had children, he'd have to keep a steady job!" It was not the lack of money, Sally insisted, but the lack of intensity and firmness in Michael, the lack of direction.

Catherine was careful not to say anything about Michael, not even to think anything about him. Married couples always had something that held them together, and in the case of Sally and Michael that something seemed to be sex. Sally's talk always turned to crude sexual jokes, as with innocent eyes and mischievous little mouth, she spurted obscenities. She used the word *fuck* constantly. Listless classmates were "little fuckers," a faulty paper was "fucked up." Everything mildly unpleasant was "fucking," and sometimes a general exclamation, "Fuck!" introduced a new subject. After a while, Catherine noticed it no more than Sally's other wiggles or tics. One day, finishing a story of a bear frightening Sally and Michael in the midst of intercourse in a sleeping bag, "...waiting for the fucking earth to shake..." Sally sighed and added, "It must be nice to be a lesbian, and not have all that goo running down your leg."

Catherine laughed. She could feel Sally watching her face. Was she watching for some reaction, or only for the laugh? Probably she was not watching at all. Her words spilled out spontaneously, meant only what they said, and meant it only for that moment. That was the way Sally talked.

While Catherine, of course, spoke as she thought, with conscientious deliberation. Certainly she did not spill out any details of her private life as Sally did. She let Sally know that she had been married once, when very young. She did not tell her about the emptiness of the marriage, the emptiness of other attempts with men, on her slow, deliberate, thoughtful way toward learning that she loved, when she loved, women. She did not tell about the five good years with Ginetta before she went back to Austria, or the lonely years since.

And in the same slow, deliberate way, Catherine learned that she loved Sally. She could not understand why. She and Sally had nothing in common, either in temperament or interests. Sally had earned a B in the class, but had no deep interest in writing or in literature. "I worked my fucking head off for Catherine, just to get a smile out of her!" Catherine dove deep into an idea, while Sally, though intelligent, danced lightly on the surface. Catherine's mind churned memories, reflections, and half-dreamed forms waiting for clarification, while Sally's every half-thought splashed and hissed out with the regularity of a steamy geyser. But Catherine decided she did not need to understand. The semester was over, Sally would take other classes, and they would gradually stop seeing each other.

She was wrong. Not only did Sally come as usual for their Saturday hike, she continued to come to Catherine's office and to call her at home. The only days which passed without some word from Sally were migraine days, occurring every week or so, when Sally lay in a dark room ". . . trying not to move a fucking finger or I'll start puking and screaming from the pain!" Catherine wanted to go to her then, when the silence told her that Sally was in pain. But it was not for her to sit with Sally and share her pain. That was Michael's privilege.

She did not know Michael any better, though she saw him often. He seemed to accept her indifferently as one of the many women friends Sally had made at the college. "Really, aren't women so much more interesting than men, and nicer!" When Michael saw Catherine, they exchanged only a few flaccid words on the subjects he was taking at the university. Evidently he was not doing well.

The first clear statement that Sally was seriously dissatisfied with her marriage came in May, during one of those blooming hot spells before the summer fog came in. It was a Tuesday evening, still light at eight-thirty. Catherine sat at her desk, reading papers. Occasionally she looked outward and down into the garden when she wanted to rest her eyes or to consider the best way to unravel a student's tangled idea.

Suddenly Sally faced her, standing outside the window, waiting, watching. Catherine jumped up and opened the door.

"Oh, I'm sorry, I should have called first. You're busy and..."

"Just papers... wishing for an excuse to quit."

They turned toward the window, toward the glow of sunset behind the shrubs and trees. "It's such a super beautiful evening, and I just needed to..." Sally's head lost its usual motion, her face went still, and tears popped out of her eyes and smeared down her cheeks. Catherine had never seen such sudden, copious tears.

"What is it? What's wrong?"

"Oh, everything!" Sally flopped down on the rug in front of the fireplace, lying prone with her outstretched fists clenched as if she would beat them on the floor. "I just want to scream and hold my breath and... have a tantrum!"

Catherine sat down on the floor, watching Sally's writhing body, waiting for her to stop crying.

"It's Michael!"

"What's he done?"

"Nothing! Nothing, nothing, nothing..." Sally sat up and pressed her fists against her head above her ears. "He hasn't done anything. He's just Michael, the same as ever, the same as he's been for ten years. Nice and quiet and loving and... I just can't stand to have him around me anymore! I think I'm going crazy. He has a midterm tomorrow, and he's sitting there reading science fiction! He's only going to school because I want him to... want him to... do something! Instead of just going on like... you know, he's going bald? I'm getting fucking gray!" She grabbed at her blonde hairs as if to pull them out, and, parting a section above her brow, she thrust her head at Catherine. "I don't want to go on waiting on table in ski lodges and lifeguarding the kiddie pool until I'm an old woman. Maybe if we'd had children. Then I wouldn't have had time to think about anything. It would be like I expected, like my mother said it was supposed to be, and I'd be too busy scraping shit off diapers, the good Catholic mother with a dozen kids!"

"But you didn't have children."

"So what do we do with our lives!"

"Well...if Michael hasn't quite decided..."

"I'm sick of waiting for him to decide. I'm sick of...oh, fuck it, Catherine, I'm sick of him! I just look at him and I can feel a migraine coming on! And I feel so guilty. He hasn't done anything wrong. He's just the same old Michael. The same. But I'm not. I want..."

Catherine waited. "You want what?"

Sally sighed and lay her head on Catherine's outstretched legs. "I don't know. A change. I have to change." She lay still and heavy, closing her eyes.

Catherine sat absolutely still. She watched her hand reach out to touch Sally's hair, stopped it, and withdrew it slowly and deliberately. She sat. After a while it was dark.

Sally raised her head. "What? I think I dozed off. Oh, Catherine, I'm sorry, I'm always coming to you with all my shit!"

"I wish I could help."

"Oh, you do help! You do. Just by being...who you are. Serene and...and capable. I mean, Catherine, you're not only in control of your life, you're...oh, you're just what I'm not! I love you, Catherine, I do. It's just like Jung says, we love the person we want to be."

"I love you too, Sally." Catherine's voice was carefully kind and bland.

"Oh, fuck!" Sally bounced up and stood swaying over Catherine, whose legs had gone to sleep. "I'm such a mess. Don't bother, I can let myself out." For a moment she stood at the door, looking around. "I love your room!" Then she turned and ran.

From that day, Sally seemed in flight from Michael, in her tearful sighs, her wriggling limbs, in her breathlessly hissed obscenities. Her body and mind thrashed with exasperation. She begged Catherine for a solution. Catherine refused to say anything. If there were to be a decision, it must be Sally's decision. So she blandly suggested adopting children, changing schools, going to a marriage counselor. She shrugged and said, "You are going through a change, and change is the hardest thing in the world." She knew she sounded pompous, but she was scared, suffering as much as Sally, fighting the arousal of hopes she had put to sleep years ago.

Catherine gave her last final exam, read her last paper, and turned in her grades in an exhausted daze. She thought she should go away

116

somewhere, but she could not gather herself to make the effort. Instead she burrowed into her garden, spending whole days on her knees, crawling inch by inch downhill, her fingers patting, probing, gripping warm, solid earth. Days passed without a word from Sally. The owner of the house had probably returned; Sally and Michael had packed up and gone. There had been talk of summer work in a hot springs resort near Calistoga. She would not hear from Sally again until next fall. Perhaps never.

Then, at sunset on the twenty-first of June, Sally appeared, throwing open the door and chanting, "Catherine, Catherine, Catherine!" She wore wide, shimmering pants and huge gold earrings. She carried two suitcases and a canvas pack. "I did it, I did! I told him. We were all packed, but I couldn't do it. I told him I wasn't going. Soon as I did, it was like a thousand-pound weight off me. And... here I am! Did you miss me?"

Catherine nodded.

"I've come to stay."

"So I see."

Sally laughed, twirled once, then giggled. "Let's celebrate. Let's go out to dinner." She grabbed Catherine's hand and led her outside, up the path along the side of the house. "What's that heavenly smell?"

"Star jasmine," said Catherine.

Sally drove to downtown Berkeley, to a tiny restaurant in an old storefront. The waitress led them through the narrow dining room, out to a garden, a square enclosed by the brick walls of neighboring buildings. Ivy zigzagged across the brick; tied-up fuchsia stems bowed over latticework frames; from the overhead branch of a dead tree drooped thin, tangled stems of clematis, still putting out broad purple flowers.

Sally giggled and shivered as they sat down at a tiny table half hidden in leafy latticework. "I'm so happy, I'm...are you happy too, Catherine?"

Catherine nodded.

"You always look so cool..."

Catherine shook her head.

"...but in your eyes, well!" Sally laughed. "You've got the most beautiful green eyes, just all kinds of stuff pouring out of them. The minute you walked into that classroom, I thought, there's the sexiest pair of eyes I ever saw!" When Catherine laughed, Sally stopped giggling and just watched her.

For the next two hours, Sally never took her eyes off Catherine. No matter how she twisted and giggled and talked, her eyes held Catherine, claimed her with a tenacity and strength Caterine had never seen in her before. As it became dark, the waitress lit a candle in an orange glass bowl. Catherine could barely see Sally's face in the dim, golden glow, and could not see her eyes at all. Sally's voice became softer, thinning into long silences. Finally she leaned forward over the glass bowl and blew out the candle. "How long are you going to make me wait?"

Catherine swallowed.

"I always wanted you," Sally hissed, "before I knew I wanted you. Why didn't you tell me? Why did we waste so much time?"

"I thought..."

"Let's not think. Let's go home."

At six in the morning Catherine lay awake, a strand of Sally's hair tickling her neck. She kept still, afraid of waking Sally. They had dozed off finally about four o'clock, but Catherine was used to getting up at six. So she had wakened after only a short sleep, wakened to find that it was all real. Sally was with her, quiet and still now, after crying out so loud at her climaxes that Catherine thought she might waken the old lady upstairs, and did not care. As for Catherine, she too was sated, not only from sex, but more with the warm, loving, smooth touch of skin against skin, breath against breath. How had she lived these past few years with no one to hold? She must be much stronger than she ever dreamed to have survived waiting so long for Sally. What human beings could endure, could live without, was a wonder. Contemplating her own strength and endurance, she fell asleep.

She awoke again at eleven and found Sally lying on her side, watching her. Sally grinned. "Hello."

"Hello."

"Are you happy?"

Catherine nodded. "You?"

Sally stretched and yawned. "Oh, like...you can't imagine how...I have to pee." She giggled and jumped up. From the bathroom she chattered through the open doorway as she urinated, laughing and saying, "I'll never stop," but Catherine could not make out what else she said. In a moment she was back, pressing her narrow body against Catherine's and pulling the blankets up around them. "My God, it's fantastic," Sally whispered. "You know...that was my first time."

"The first time you made love with a woman."

Sally shook her head. "No. I mean, yes, I never made love with a woman, or with anyone but Michael, but I mean...the first time I ever got there. Climaxed. I mean, I didn't know what an orgasm was! I used to just get sort of tired after a while, and I thought... well, if you don't know what something is, you don't know if you don't have it."

Catherine shook her head. "The way you always talked, I thought..."

"Well, you know what they say about the people who talk about it the most!"

Catherine laughed.

"So, you see, I came to you a virgin." Sally nuzzled her head into Catherine's neck and blew on it. "But I catch on fast."

"You certainly do," said Catherine, dipping her chin to take the the deep kiss that would begin it all again.

They settled quickly into a routine that was unplanned but seemed as inevitable as the growth of a plant from a seed. Early every morning they set out in the fog, hiking up over the hills. They returned home in sunshine, to eat a long slow breakfast of fruit and cheese in the garden. Then Sally went out to shop, leaving Catherine alone, "...so you'll miss me." Catherine welcomed the few hours of silence, for she had begun to write poems again. Sometimes, working at her desk at the window, she did not even notice Sally's return, but found her later sitting quietly on the floor beside her. Then Catherine worked in the garden while Sally cooked dinner. In the evenings they read or listened to records. They went to bed early, not only to make love but to talk.

Catherine told Sally things about herself that she had never told anyone, not even Ginetta, because she never really knew them before. "You know," she explained, "whatever happens changes with time. As time passes, you know more and more deeply the meaning of what happened. And that changes it."

Sally shrugged and shook her head. Her mind did not work that way. She told Catherine about events and her feelings during the events, but there was no development in her thought. "Like I said, I'm shallow."

"Spontaneous."

Sally shook her head, her hair brushing against Catherine's cheek in the dark. "I'll never be able to catch up with you, no matter how much I read."

"We're not in a race, dear."

"I don't think I'll ever be like you!"

"I wouldn't want you to be."

Letters began to come from Michael. "They're all the same. He loves me. He misses me. When am I coming up." Sally threw the latest in the fireplace.

"Perhaps you should answer."

"No!" Sally began to twitch and sway every time she talked about Michael. "I told him when he left that we were through. But he acts like I never said it. He always did that, acted like I didn't say whatever he didn't want to hear. I could say something so awful you'd think he'd just die, and he'd act like I never said it. He just didn't listen." They were sitting at breakfast in bathing suits, and Sally was blotting up a streak of yogurt spilled on her chest. "You know, I haven't had a migraine since..." Tears filled her eyes. "Oh, Catherine, you are really my first love. We belong together."

The next day Sally returned from shopping while Catherine was still writing, tiptoeing in and then quickly dashing to answer the phone at the first ring. Catherine felt her concentration pierced by Sally's tense silences between short phrases. "...well, you know... no...because I don't...no, I can't...oh, look Michael...no... well, because I...oh, all right...all right!" She slammed down the receiver as she snapped, "Oh, fuck!" Catherine waited. "He was crying. He believes me. Finally. Wants to talk to me. Wants me to come up this weekend so we can talk things over. Friday night. Is that tomorrow? Oh, shit!"

"I guess you have to settle things sooner or later."

Sally's head bobbed. "I know. I just wish it was over. He keeps saying, 'You just can't throw ten years of marriage away,' and the fucker, he wrote to my mother. She'll have the Church, Mother Mary, and all the saints down on me!" She blinked her eyes. "Oh, God, my head, I can feel it coming!"

Catherine massaged Sally's neck and gave her camomile tea. Sally lay with her eyes covered for an hour, then sat up. "It's still there, but hasn't got me yet. It's waiting. One false move and it'll grab me." She smiled wanly. "I'm such a fucking coward."

That night Sally slept restlessly, her twitching and wiggling reminding Catherine how much more quiet she had been during the
past few weeks. When she moaned, Catherine held her, and when
they woke in the morning it was Catherine who was tired, while
Sally smiled, nearly glowing with relaxed, calm determination.
"It'll be okay, you'll see. No, no headache. You made it go away.
That's the first time, ever." She sighed. "It just has to be done."

They spent the day as usual, walking, nibbling at their long breakfast, and when Catherine sat down to write, Sally stuffed a few
clothes into her canvas pack, then went out to have her car checked
and gassed.

They ate an early dinner at the garden restaurant. This time they
talked about their future, and Sally seemed quite mature and
resolute.

"You really think I am? I'm just gritting my teeth, and it makes
me look grown up for a change. But will you still love me if I
grow up?"

"More than ever," said Catherine.

Sally bit her lip. "I still don't think it's fair that I shouldn't work,
at least part time. I could. . ."

"We settled all that." Catherine shook her head. "At least for
the first year. I make much more money than I need. Later, when
you transfer to the university, when you know. . ."

". . . what I'm going to be when I grow up!"

"And next week, we'll start looking for a house. We'll need more
space, and I've been meaning to get out of that room and buy
something."

They went home while it was still light. Sally undressed Catherine and made love to her, insisting on dominance, making Catherine
sink into a dreamy passivity from which Sally roused her again and
again, laughing like a child proud of new learning, new power.

Then Catherine lay on the sofa-bed while Sally showered and
dressed in shabby jeans and a striped shirt with a hole at the elbow.
"I'm going to get it over with tonight and come back tomorrow. I
couldn't stand a whole weekend. I'll call you in the morning. Okay?"
Catherine nodded and watched Sally move to the door where her
canvas pack lay. She tripped over it, whispered one final, "fuck!"
then turned to look back at Catherine. But the light of the sunset
shone behind her head so that Catherine could not see her expression.

The next morning Catherine awoke as usual at six. She layered records on the phonograph and set it going. She defrosted the refrigerator, scrubbed the oven, and mopped the kitchen floor. Then she began to shelve the books that were lying around everywhere, books that Sally had picked up and tried, then laid down. After lunch she washed the panes of the window wall, inside and out. She spent the late afternoon working in the garden. The phone rang twice, friends inviting her to a concert and complaining that they never saw her anymore. That night she read, or tried to read. She went to bed early.

On Sunday morning she awoke remembering an old movie in which a girl is hit by a car on the way to meet her lover, and, crippled for life, lets him think he has been jilted. She knew that such neat, sentimental catastrophes happened only in movies. The catastrophe she saw rolling toward her was dirty and mean. She lay on the sofa-bed most of the morning and spent the rest of the day sitting at her desk, looking numbly through the clean, invisible window panes.

By Sunday night, there was no doubt left, but she nevertheless lay awake most of the night, listening for the sound of someone on the path beside the house. Near dawn, she fell into a doze, from which she dragged herself at about ten in the morning.

Monday afternoon she pulled Sally's two suitcases out of the closet and began to pack her clothes. Then she found a large box for all the things that would not fit into the suitcases: books, records, scented candles which lay around unused after Catherine protested the first whiff of one, jars and bottles full of lotions and creams, an omelette pan, two posters, and dozens of little scraps Sally had cut from magazines and pinned to the walls. Catherine put the suitcases and the box near the door, where they stayed through Wednesday.

She is afraid to come while I'm here, thought Catherine. Thursday morning she left the house early, spent the morning in the library, then met a friend for lunch. When she went back to her car, it would not start. She almost welcomed the frustration, complaining to the man who towed her, to her mechanic, to the woman she sat next to on the bus she took home. It felt good to complain about a misfortune that everyone understood, everyone would sympathize with. When she got home, Sally's things were still by the door.

At about ten that night, she heard the rustle of the bushes on the side of the house. She looked up from her book and waited. By the time the door opened, her heart was shaking her with deep, rapid thuds. Sally's head waved and bobbed. "Oh, I thought you were out... didn't see your car."

"Your things are there, by the door."

"Oh, yes, thanks." Sally stood swaying, her mouth making uncertain, inconclusive shapes. "I was going to call, but..."

"Don't explain," Catherine said abruptly.

"Oh, I knew you would understand!" Sally's mouth relaxed and made its smile. She was moving into the room, her mouth working, her hands twitching at her sides. "You do understand! It was... so different. We talked! He understands things better, and I understand him. I mean, there are things men just can't say, can't express their feelings, poor things, but he tried for once, and told me all sorts of thoughts and things I never knew he... well, he really has suffered, poor Michael." She was still for a moment, then, seeing that Catherine would not respond, she went on. "You can't just throw away ten years of marriage. I haven't always been perfect either, and Michael has always been so patient. I mean, ten years!"

"You said that."

"And all the time our trouble was so simple, if we only knew." She had moved closer and was leaning against Catherine's desk. "We were married so young. I didn't know anything, and Michael never had much experience either, so he just didn't know."

"You mean sex." Catherine sat holding her knees, gripping each one with a cupped hand, holding on as her fingers spread, digging her fingers into the flesh. "You told him."

"Yes, you see, he didn't know. He thought it was all just shoving in and out, and when I showed him how easy... well, it's no big thing, is it, anybody can learn..."

"And he did."

Sally sighed a long, hissing, "Yesss. And then we talked. The way we never could before. You know, how you do, after..."

Catherine stared, incredulous, at Sally's complacent, self-absorbed face.

"Really, we have you to thank. Michael said that. And he's right, you know you really saved our marriage. If it hadn't been for you..."

"Michael said that?"

123

Sally nodded, smiling.

"You told him everything. And he wasn't jealous?"

Sally laughed. "Not at all."

"Why not?"

"Huh?"

"I said, why not!" Catherine shouted hoarsely.

"Uh..." Sally was frowning, almost squinting, as if to see Catherine more clearly. "I'm a little dim...just getting over a migraine...I don't know what you mean about..."

"Why wasn't he jealous?" Catherine stood and turned her back on Sally, facing the dead fireplace. "You left him for me. You had better sex with me. Better everything. I'm more intelligent than he is, more understanding, more accomplished, more dependable, more interested in your development. Yet he isn't jealous. Why! Because I'm a woman? Only a woman, so I don't count. Like you, Sally, I'm only a woman, so what I do and say and feel isn't to be taken seriously." She turned to face Sally, who had backed up along side of the desk and now stood against the window, like a child taking a scolding, hoping to be dismissed soon. "And you too! You could play around with me because I don't count. It wasn't really cheating, it wasn't serious, because it was only with a woman!"

Sally gave a little wiggling shrug and smiled placatingly. "Oh, Catherine, I could never be a lesbian, I have too much respect for women, for you. I'm just in awe of you. I can't be myself the way I am with Michael. I'm really awful sometimes, and he puts up with all kinds of shit that you wouldn't!"

"But that was what you were running away from! You wanted to change! You didn't want his condescension, his..."

"You should just see this darling old hot springs these new owners are fixing up. We can stay at least a year, hiking and taking the baths and all, just for working on the place, helping rebuild. I've missed the country. Berkeley is so crowded. As soon as I got there, I knew..."

"And what about school?"

"Oh, I enjoyed that! I'll never forget all I learned from you. I mean, how you really taught me to think! But, I told you, I'm really shallow, I could never be like you."

"I never wanted you to be like me. I wanted you to become yourself!" She leaned on the desk, held on to it.

Sally shrugged and edged toward the door. "I am. This is all I am."

"And what about me? Me! Did you ever think that you had any responsibility toward me?"

"Oh, Catherine, you don't know!" Sally whispered. "I've just been so miserable. Whenever I thought about you, I just felt awful. Just sick. Really, I just feel..."

"You feel! You feel! Is that all you know is how you feel!"

"Look, I have to go, Michael's waiting in the car...but pretty soon...when you feel...maybe next month or anytime, really, we want you to come and visit us. Michael said it, he suggested it. He really likes you, and respects you too, he said..."

Catherine never heard what Michael had said about her, for she lost her grip on the desk and her body dived forward, her hands aimed at Sally's long, throbbing throat, her own throat torn by a howl of rage.

But Sally, as Catherine knew, was stronger than she looked. With one long, straight arm, the heel of her hand meeting Catherine's chest, she stopped her. A slight push, and Catherine fell to the floor, where finally the tears came, shaking her body with sobs that turned to dry retching. When she looked up again, Sally was gone.

During the next few days her body ached as if she had been beaten. But more painful was the feverish writhing of her mind. Mired in rage, it rehearsed more confrontations with Sally, twisting through every possible variation of every possible condemnation. She mumbled denunciations. She sat and wrote long, bitter letters to Sally. The unmailed letters piled up on the desk. At night she tossed in bed, crying and cursing.

But gradually her old consciousness returned. She saw her mind wallowing in rage and self-pity, and she yanked it out. She saw friends. She read. She worked in the garden. She began to gather materials for the fall semester.

In the darkening August mornings, she sat at her desk, taking in the long, downhill view and seeing her life like the conclusion of a story. She would go back to what had been, back to reading the half-thoughts of young people who feared thinking, back to working in her garden. She would buy a big house, as her friends urged, where she could pour all the extra money and energy and love that had nowhere else to go. That was the way stories like hers ended. She had read them all, and she knew.

But when classes began again, she found herself unable to face them. Something in her had snapped, cracked, or simply melted. She had lost the will to look into those shifting, frightened, hard eyes. Rows and rows of them. They paralyzed her.

She took sick leave and went back to sitting before the big window, looking down into the garden.

One morning she tried clearing her desk, picking up the angry letters to throw them away. A phrase caught her eye. She sat down and copied it on a clean sheet of paper. It needed another. And then another. They came as fast as she could write, and when they stopped coming, she settled down to the long, slow, deliberate shaping and reshaping.

She never went back to teaching, and she never bought a big house. By the time her savings ran out, she had acquired enough afternoons of gardening work to pay her few expenses. Her poems began to appear in magazines again, and one critic described hers as "a voice of passionate deliberation." Recently she won a prize for a collection published under the title *Changes*. The dedication page reads, "In all fairness, to Sally."

DELILAH
A One-Act Play

I wrote this play in 1973. Its few "performances" were those instigated by my friend Betty Bacon, who frequently would insist that she and my husband and I read it to unsuspecting friends who came to dinner. At their suggestion I added the prologue for the benefit of people who have never read the biblical account.

My play proceeds from two unchallenged elements of the Bible myth: that Delilah was a Philistine woman and that she must have been a prostitute. As a Philistine, she was an enemy of the Hebrew Samson, not the betrayer of a trusting lover, but a paid political spy. As a prostitute who could be approached by Samson, she was an outcast among the Philistines. Since she proved an effective spy, we may assume her intelligence. That intelligence would have led to ambivalent thoughts about disarming an enemy who represented another outcast group, slaves of the Philistines.

Terinah is the name I have given to another character briefly mentioned in the Bible, Samson's sister-in-law. After the destruction of her home and family, it is possible that she too would have become an outcast.

The messenger is an invented character, but a familiar one.

The play can be performed in any space, the closer to the audience, the better. The three actors will need two tall stools, a few props, easily assembled modern costumes, and one entry/exit.

Prologue

(TERINAH enters carrying a large Bible. She is a young woman, dressed seductively in what is obviously the garb of a prostitute. She wears plenty of make-up and jewelry. Nothing soft about her; she is angry and hurt. She is always aware of the audience and directs much of what she says to them. She often glances at the audience to watch their reaction. She sits on one of the stools, shows the title of the book to the audience. She opens the Bible, finds her place, and begins to read aloud. As she reads, she makes appropriate personal reactions, as an anonymous, forgotten victim in the story she is reading. As she begins reading, her tone is cool, skeptical, unimpressed, but not sarcastic.)

TERINAH

"And the children of Israel did evil in the sight of the Lord; and the Lord delivered them into the hand of the Philistines forty years. And there was a certain man whose wife was barren. And the angel of the Lord appeared unto her. Lo, thou shalt conceive and bear a son; and no razor shall come on his head; for the child shall be a Nazarite unto God from the womb; and he shall begin to deliver Israel out of the hand of the Philistines."

(She reads silently for a moment.) "And the woman bare a son and called his name Samson. And the child grew, and the Lord blessed him." *(She reads silently, turns the page.)* "And Samson saw a woman in Timnath of the daughters of the Philistines. And he came up and told his father and his mother, I have seen a woman of the daughters of the Philistines; now therefore get her for me to wife. Then his father and his mother said unto him, Is there never a woman among the daughters of thy brethren, or among all my people, that thou goes to take a wife of the uncircumcised Philistines? And Samson said unto his father, Get her for me, for she pleaseth me well."

(Looks angry, reads silently for a while.)

"And at the wedding feast Samson put forth a riddle to the Philistine men. . . and they could not in three days expound the riddle. On the seventh day of the feast they said unto Samson's wife, Entice thy husband, that he may declare unto us the riddle, lest we burn thee and thy father's house with fire."

(Looks stricken, as if she might cry, but then gains control and goes on.) "And she wept before him until he told her. And the Philistines expounded the riddle. Then Samson's anger was kindled, and he went down to Ashkelon and he slew thirty men." *(She reads on silently.)*

"And later Samson came back to his wife, but her father said, I thought thou utterly hated her, therefore I gave her to thy companion: is not her younger sister fairer than she? Take her." *(TERINAH is angry to the point of fury. She pauses to get control of herself.)*

"So Samson went and caught three hundred foxes, and put firebrands on their tails. And when he had set the brands on fire, he let them go into the standing corn of the Philistines, and burnt up both the shocks, the standing corn, the vineyards, and the olives." *(Now her voice should begin low, growing in sadness until she is crying.)*

"Then the Philistines said, Who hath done this? And they answered, Samson, the son-in-law of the Timnite, because he had taken his wife, and given her to his companion. And the Philistines came up, and burnt her and her father with fire." *(Gradually she stops crying, then goes on grimly, but with no satisfaction at the slaughter.)*

"And Samson said, I will be avenged of you, and he smote them hip and thigh, with great slaughter. And the Philistines pursued him, and he found a new jawbone of an ass, and put forth his hand, and took it, and slew a thousand men therewith."

(Reads silently, then looks up at audience.) There's a lot more of this kind of thing. *(Reads silently, turns the page. Looks up at audience again before going on, slowly, portentously.)*

"And it came to pass afterward that he loved a woman whose name was Delilah. And the lords of the Philistines came up into her and said unto her, Entice him, and see wherein his great strength lieth, and by what means we may prevail against him, that we may bind him and afflict him: and we will give thee everyone of us eleven hundred pieces of silver.'' *(She looks at the audience, then closes the book.)* Of course, you know the rest of this story. Or you think you do. *(She puts the book down and begins brushing her hair, filing her nails, or any other chronic grooming action that shows not so much vanity as nerves constantly on edge.)*

The Play

(DELILAH enters. She is older than TERINAH, at least thirty. Strong face, minimal make-up and jewelry, simple clothes, maybe pants. Her beauty lies in a look of thoughtful intelligence mixed with hope. She has often been sad, but not cynical. She occasionally addresses the audience, but is not so constantly aware of them as TERINAH is.)

TERINAH

(Still grooming, hardly looks up.) Are they still celebrating?

DELILAH

(Nods.) The streets are full of drunks.

TERINAH

(Shakes her head.) When I think of the money we could be making. . .

DELILAH

That's all over, Terinah. Never another man for money. Never again. You don't believe me.

TERINAH

If it's true, why aren't *we* celebrating?

DELILAH

I don't feel like celebrating. I feel. . .it was a dirty business.

TERINAH

Well, it's over with and done. Forget it.

DELILAH

If only it could have been a clean fight. As men fight. If I could have attacked him, face to face, directly, and killed him...then I'd feel like celebrating. Like a soldier who had defended his country. A soldier home from battle. *(As she finishes, she realizes that what she says might sound amusing. She is serious, but does not take herself so seriously as to be a prig.)*

TERINAH

(To audience.) As a man? As a soldier? *(To DELILAH.)* Come, Delilah, we've known enough soldiers to know better. The only time men fight face to face, direct and honest, is when they're drunk, brawling over something that doesn't matter. In the important battles they use bribes and spies and...women like us.

DELILAH

I suppose you're right. Yet...I always dreamed of struggling for something fine, fighting a good fight, a just fight. Doing something important, something...useful.

TERINAH

Well, you did. You were terrific! I'll never forget the look on his stupid face when...

DELILAH

Don't! No. Don't remind me of it. I don't want to think about it. *(There is a knock from the entry.)*
That must be them. Come in.

TERINAH

Well, it's about time. *(She primps a bit as she looks toward the entry, but does not look pleased.)*

(MESSENGER enters and looks around. A young man, about thirty. He is good-looking and well-dressed, like a model in a television ad. He is polite, charming, intelligent, overeducated for his

132

job. He likes to think of himself as identifying with interesting out-siders like DELILAH, while maintaining his place in the Establish-ment. He is anxious to please and to smooth over awkward situa-tions. That is his job, and he takes pride in doing it well. He carries an attache case. He shows no awareness of the audience until his final speech. Flashes of humanity occasionally break through his charming shell. He immediately recognizes DELILAH and nods politely to her. He sets his attache case down on a stool, opens it, and pulls out a wad of paper currency, which he holds out to DELILAH.)

DELILAH
(Not taking the money.) What is this? Who are you?

MESSENGER
(Continues to hold out the money.) You are Delilah? I come on the highest authority to give you . . .

DELILAH
The generals sent you?

MESSENGER
Yes, madam.

DELILAH
To give me this money.

MESSENGER
Yes, madam.

DELILAH
What did they say?

MESSENGER
That I was to deliver this money to the woman, Delilah, for . . . ser-vices rendered.

DELILAH

Go on.

MESSENGER

That's all.

DELILAH

That's all? They said nothing more?

MESSENGER

Nothing.

DELILAH

(Conflicting emotions pass over her face. Perhaps she looks at TERINAH, who would make some gesture of I-told-you-so anger; perhaps she looks at audience. Finally she gains control and turns back to MESSENGER.) There has been a mistake. A misunderstanding. They must have...forgotten our agreement. Go back and remind the generals that they must all come here to... deliver payment. Do you understand?

MESSENGER

Yes, madam. Shall I leave the money?

DELILAH

No! *(More quietly.)* No. Take it back, give it to them, tell them... tell them to come.

MESSENGER

Now?

DELILAH

Yes. Now.

MESSENGER

(Smiles condescendingly.) Madam, you realize, of course, that the generals are very busy men, and that...

DELILAH

Now!

MESSENGER

(Shrugs.) Very well, madam. I'll tell them, but...(Packs up his attache case and exits.)

TERINAH

You should have taken the money. That's all you'll ever get out of it. I told you. Now you'll probably lose even the money.

DELILAH

I don't care about the money. I did...

TERINAH

Yes, I know. You did it for the people. For honor. The good fight. You did their dirty work for them because you thought you could win their respect. Oh, Delilah, what a child you are. I told you, women like us can never...

DELILAH

Stop saying "women like us." Respect yourself. We are human beings, just like...

TERINAH

Not if they don't treat us like human beings.

DELILAH

Yes! Yes, no matter what they do or say. I may have to sell my body, but I never sell my mind. I have never thought as a whore.

TERINAH

You'd be smarter if you did. Any whore knows better than to think she wins the respect of a man by doing what his wife won't do.

DELILAH

How can you compare what I did to...

135

TERINAH

I'm only trying to wake you up! Trying to make you see what you already know. . .what you know about all these people you agreed to save.

DELILAH

Did save!

TERINAH

All right, did save. But you should have known what thanks you'd get. You were lucky they even sent the money. Haven't I told you over and over. . .Delilah, it was our own people, it was the Philistines who killed my father and my sister. Killed their own kind. And you expected those butchers to keep their word to you!

DELILAH

But you were the one who urged me to do it. When I refused, you said. . .

TERINAH

I wanted to see Samson's face when they carried him off. I wanted to ask him, Do you know me now? Do you recognize me, changed as I am by what you did? Now do you know how it feels to be abandoned as you abandoned my sister? Oh, I would have gone to watch that. I would have stood in the front row! I would have set the torch. . .
(During this speech the MESSENGER has quietly re-entered. He listens impassively, but DELILAH grows more and more uneasy.)

DELILAH

Stop, Terinah, stop that. You only hurt yourself when you. . .*(She sees the MESSENGER, who has again put his attache case on the stool and is opening it.)*

MESSENGER

The generals have asked me to convey to you their very sincere regrets that they are unable to come.

136

TERINAH

They were able to come before. They hid for hours in the next room, waiting for her to disarm Samson, so they could take him. *(To DE-LILAH.)* They came when they needed something from you. They have it now. They won't come again.

MESSENGER

I am fully empowered to represent them. *(He reaches into attache case.)* And I quite agree with you that the amount of money is not sufficient. I am, therefore, instructed to double it!

DELILAH

I don't want your money!

MESSENGER

I suggest you take it, madam. The amount will not be further increased. This is absolutely the highest...

TERINAH

Give it here. I'll take it for her.
(MESSENGER hesitates, then crosses and hands money to TERINAH.)

DELILAH

(Turns on him furiously.) But that was not the agreement!

MESSENGER

(Nods sympathetically. It is clearly part of his job to listen, to smooth over difficult situations, to soothe angry, frustrated people.) Why don't you tell me all about it. *(He sits down on the stool, prepared to listen.)* Perhaps I could help to clear up any misunderstanding...

TERINAH

(Laughs.) Misunderstanding!

DELILAH

(Looks at him for a moment. More curiosity than indignation.) Just what do you think I am?

MESSENGER

(Looks her up and down appreciatively.) An intelligent, unusual, attractive woman, who through no fault of hers, occupies a low position...

TERINAH

Not so low as you!

DELILAH

I chose not to live as the wife of a Philistine. There was only one other way for me to live. So be it. I live among outcasts, earning my living the only way your generals will let me. But when Samson came here, I would have turned him away. My condition is not so low that I would receive an infamous enemy of our people.

TERINAH

Our people! *(Muttered more to herself than to anyone else.)*

DELILAH

And there were personal reasons. My friend Terinah was gravely injured by Samson. He married her sister, and then...well, it is a long story. Because of Samson, Terinah has lost her family and her chance for a decent place among our people. I would not allow him near the doorway. Not if I had been starving! And then...the generals came. Wearing their decorations, followed by their sycophants and their servants and...

MESSENGER

Yes, madam, I was among the...staff people.

DELILAH

You came with them? I don't remember you.

MESSENGER

I am paid to be efficient, not conspicuous. It is my job to listen, to carry out orders, at times to offer advice.

DELILAH

Then you heard. You heard them ask me to spy for them, to receive Samson here, to find out the secret of his strength, to disarm him, so they could take him and destroy him.

MESSENGER

Yes, ma'am, I heard.

DELILAH

Then you must have heard me refuse.

MESSENGER

Yes, I did. I never understood that. First you said you hated him, then you refused to help the generals capture him.

DELILAH

It was simple enough. I'm a bad liar. When I lie, my whole body rebels. I make little movements, gestures, faces, that tell I am lying. It was refusing to lie that made me an outcast.

MESSENGER

Yet, in your profession...

DELILAH

I never lie! I sell my services at a fair price. Without apology. With ...a certain style, perhaps. But never to a man I despise. Never with lies. I told them I wouldn't be any good at it. To get someone else. There are plenty who...

TERINAH

You wouldn't have had to be good at lying. Samson is so stupid and vain...

MESSENGER

But Samson wanted you. As I can well understand. *(His little attempt at gallantry falls flat as DELILAH glares at him.)* Sorry, I only meant to...

DELILAH

So they offered me more money.

MESSENGER

Quite a bit more. But I could see you weren't listening. It was I who took one of them aside and told him you were the type who wouldn't be bought by money. That they'd have to find something else...

TERINAH

And then the speech-making started.

MESSENGER

Yes. To tell the truth I didn't listen very closely to that part. They make those same speeches over and over...

DELILAH

They told me they understood my aversion and admired me for it. But that I must try to overcome it, try to think of my country, my people. They told how many he had killed, how many children starved when he burned the crops, how many more he had sworn to kill. That they could not stop him, with all their men and weapons. But that I, a single woman, I alone might be able to save my people.

TERINAH

(To audience.) Save her people! Women who will not speak to her, children who snicker and throw things when she passes them on the street, men who rent her as a convenience. Her people!

DELILAH

Yet you urged me to do it, Terinah.

TERINAH

For money and revenge, the two realities. Not for any fine words. You understood me.

DELILAH

Yes, I understood you, but your arguments meant less than theirs.
It was when I thought about the children...

TERINAH

Children are just smaller Philistines. They grow up to be like their
parents.

DELILAH

But they might not, if they were not so badly taught. If they could
be shown that we are all human beings, if...

MESSENGER

Yes, ma'am, I started listening again, when you started talking.
You were very eloquent, though you had to repeat yourself over
and over before they understood what you wanted.

DELILAH

But finally they did. You admit that. You admit there was no misunderstanding. They offered me...respect. Said they would an-
nounce what I had done, make it known to the people, even honor
me in some kind of ceremony. But I didn't want any ceremonies,
just...

TERINAH

And they had no intention of giving any. They don't want anyone
to know what you did. You've heard the story in the streets, how
the generals overcame Samson, the brave generals...

DELILAH

I don't care. Let them tell whatever stories they want. I'd be glad
to forget my part in it. I didn't ask for honors or ceremonies. I asked
for work. For some way to earn my living doing a decent, respectable service to my people. It was simple enough, much less than all
this money. Do you remember?

MESSENGER

Yes, I remember every word. Because it seemed so strange. Made me think. I'd never heard such a strange thing. How could you ask to do or be what you are not? I mean. . . women are wives or whores, just as Hebrews are slaves, just as beggars are beggars, and. . .

DELILAH

You talk as if you are describing the order of the universe, the movements of the planets. . .

MESSENGER

Yes, I never questioned any of it, until I heard you queston it.

DELILAH

You have questioned it since?

MESSENGER

(A little too vehemently.) No! *(More quietly, uneasily.)* I learned. . . long ago. . . I learned not to let myself ask. . . troublesome questions. But, I admit, I have been. . . troubled. . . since. . . *(He recovers, becomes quite brisk.)*

Now, madam, let me be perfectly honest with you. Slaves and outcasts are used frequently to rescue our society. I might even say that our way of life depends upon continual, quiet sacrifice by the lower orders. Now. From time to time, a lucky outcast or slave has the opportunity to perform an even greater service to the state, one that calls for a very great reward. One that might even raise the outcast to a very favored position. . . very discreetly, of course. You are one of those lucky outcasts. That is really a very considerable amount of money your friend is holding, and I'll admit I was empowered to add even more to it, if necessary. Here. *(He reaches into the attache case, pulls out another pack of bills and throws it to TERINAH.)* I'll tell them you drove a hard bargain. But money is all you'll get, madam. Be realistic. You can't expect the government to rehabilitate you. That would be expecting them to overturn all our values, to turn over the whole social order. If they did that, why, they wouldn't be a government anymore, would they?

142

(He laughs uncomfortably, as if a bit shocked by the conclusion he has reached. He may even look around as if afraid he may have been overheard.)

TERINAH

(Laughing at him and at what he has said.) Then it really was a misunderstanding. Because the generals are incapable of understanding a word she said. I bet after they left here, they had a good laugh. *(A moment of uncomfortable silence confirms what TERINAH has said.)*

MESSENGER

I didn't laugh.

TERINAH

(To DELILAH.) You talked to them as if they were just men, asking you to help save a just society. But if there were a just society, run by just men, would you and I be whores? Would Hebrews be slaves? Would my sister have been given to a slave and then burned? Would there even be a Samson?

MESSENGER

Your friend is quite right. You were asking corrupt, selfish, exploitive men to become just, fair, and good. *(He smiles and shakes his head.)*

DELILAH

You can say that and still serve them?

MESSENGER

Madam, we all serve them, whether we know it or not.

DELILAH

And I've been deluding myself. . . in thinking any other way was possible.

MESSENGER

I never delude myself. I gave up such luxuries. I grew up. That means facing reality. Like your friend here. Don't think you are the only person ever to have ideals. I'm not what you think. I'm really a...a poet. If I only had the time, I would...*(He looks defiantly at TERINAH, who has burst out laughing again at this.)* Yes! I used to write long epics about the heroes of our legends...strong men...brave women...*(His voice has become dreamy, carried away in nostalgia and sentimentality. Now he recovers himself, clears his throat, looks businesslike.)* Then it was time to...to grow up. I took a good, long look at our society. I appraised it...realistically!...and then I made for myself a very comfortable place in it. I suggest you do the same. There's enough money there for you to open a large house. You wouldn't have to...receive men yourself anymore. You could live very comfortably.

TERINAH

As comfortably as the wives of the generals, without having to sleep with them.

DELILAH

That is your best offer.

MESSENGER

The very best. Better than most people get.

DELILAH

So. *(To audience.)* I have gotten exactly what I deserve. What a vain fool I was. Easily as vain and stupid as Samson ever was. I wanted to be a hero. I wanted to rise to a place of respect among my people. And all I have done is to sink lower than any whore. A hired assassin. I did everything but draw the knife. I murdered for money.

MESSENGER

I wouldn't put it quite that strongly. He's not dead yet, after all.

144

DELILAH

Not dead?

MESSENGER

Not yet. Oh, he'll be executed eventually, but not killed right off. That's not the way the government does things. First there is the interrogation...

DELILAH

Interrogation? What for?

TERINAH

He means torture.

DELILAH

But why? What could he tell them?

MESSENGER

In this case, nothing. He acted alone, and he never denied his crimes, boasted of them, in fact.

DELILAH

Then why...

MESSENGER

Interrogation is...customary. The prisoner lists his crimes, sees the error of his ways, begs pardon...

TERINAH

Samson! Beg pardon of the Philistines!

MESSENGER

Well, they couldn't get him to...I told them this was different from a case where a man wouldn't admit to the charges, wouldn't give names. And that they'd have a hard time getting Samson to show any...regrets for what he'd done.

DELILAH

Senseless torture!

MESSENGER

Yes, ma'am, that's exactly what it was. I said as much as I could, but it doesn't pay to interfere with the interrogators. They're really ...well, they give me the creeps. Even the generals don't question their methods, as long as they get results.

DELILAH

And did they get...results? Did Samson write a confession, an apology?

TERINAH

He can't write his own name, let alone anything else.

MESSENGER

No. He was very stubborn...unfortunately for him.

DELILAH

What did they do to him?

MESSENGER

(Pause.) You wouldn't want to know the details. I can tell you this: he's still alive, still in...one piece. The broken bones will mend. Oh...his sight won't come back.

TERINAH

Blind!

DELILAH

(She makes a sick, disgusted sound.) I met the enemy and defeated him. A clean kill. It should have been a clean kill! Oh, how filthy.

MESSENGER

I understand.

146

DELILAH

(Puzzled.) You do?

MESSENGER

Yes, of course, for a woman...

DELILAH

For a woman? What do you mean?

MESSENGER

Why...that you fell in love with him.

DELILAH

(Completely mystified.) With who?

MESSENGER

Why, with Samson. It is quite understandable. The man has a certain animal vitality, an appeal to...

TERINAH

OooaaAAH *(She rises with a cry somewhere between a growl and a howl of rage. She looks as if she would tear into him. She may even do so, but then is quieted and restrained by DELILAH.)*

DELILAH

(Quietly and evenly.) I could no more love Samson than I could love...you. In fact, yes, he is very like you. Very.

TERINAH

(Laughs.) Like him?

DELILAH

(Deliberately, thoughtfully.) Yes, like him. Philistine.

MESSENGER

Samson, a Philistine? Madam, I really don't...

DELILAH

Of course, in his heart. Yes. That is why he insisted on marrying Terinah's sister, a Philistine woman. And that is why he pursued me instead of a Hebrew woman. Isn't it obvious? He wanted what Philistine men have. And everything else about him was no different from the men I have known all my life, even to his boasting that he was superior, that some god was on his side, and that this god inspired him in every childish loss of temper, every selfish act, every destructive impulse.

TERINAH

(Nodding.) You mean how, afterward, they all doze off, telling you they always knew from the time they were born that they were special, different, unique. *(Thoughtfully—softening.)* I used to believe that too, when I was a very little girl. I thought I was...special. *(Hard again.)* But I got over it.

DELILAH

His vanity. His childish little tricks to show his strength. The riddles to try to make others feel as stupid as he feared he was. His pride in killing, destroying, not to try to free his people, no, but in simple, peevish anger at a slight to his pride. And, you know, I didn't have to coax the secret of his strength from him. I had only to sit still and listen, while he spilled everything. Boasting. Samson was a slave and a son of slaves. In his heart he wanted, not to be free, but merely to be a master instead of a slave. Yes, in his heart he was a Philistine. And you think I could love him!

MESSENGER

(Remains still, gazing at her in admiration. Then he nods with real respect.) I apologize, madam.

TERINAH

(Thoughtfully.) Samson blind! How fitting. How absolutely right.

DELILAH

What will they do to him now? More torture?

148

MESSENGER

No, they've given up on that. He's awaiting trial.

DELILAH

Trial!?

TERINAH

(Laughs almost hysterically.) Oh, my God, yes. Everyone has the right to a trial.

MESSENGER

A public trial. That's quite right. It's all going to be done properly. He'll be tried and then executed. *(A bit ironic. He's become rather friendly toward DELILAH now.)*

DELILAH

And when will this... trial take place?

MESSENGER

Oh, not for a while. Not until... well, until he can at least stand up again. It's going to be a very grand affair. We're still trying to find a large enough hall to accommodate the public. We may have to build one. That's my idea. It has the advantage of creating employment. You see, the government wants to get maximum political value from the trial. The people have been... uneasy lately, but now the generals have had their great victory, and the trial is needed to top it off, to consolidate power. Everything takes time. Even after we build the hall, it's going to take forever to settle the seating arrangements. I always get thankless jobs like that. Already the generals' wives are quarreling about seniority and titles in the seating. Oh, no, I don't think we'll come to trial before next spring.

DELILAH

(Quietly and slowly.) That long.

MESSENGER

Oh, at least.
(DELILAH begins to laugh, at first silently, then aloud. The MES-
SENGER watches her uneasily.)
Oh, you needn't appear at the trial. You're not expected to testify.
Your part in this...as your friend says...is not to be mentioned.
The generals want to take all the credit.

DELILAH

(While he has been talking, her laughter has subsided. She is facing
away from him. She wheels around to face him.) Listen. You go
back to your generals and tell them that they are not through with
me yet. Tell them I have information. Vital information. Tell them
that without this information, they will lose their victory, perhaps
even their lives. Unless I give them this information, they will bring
destruction upon themselves, upon everyone. But this time, they
will get their information on my terms...my terms, do you understand that? They will come here, now, with all their decorations
and their flunkies...

TERINAH

And their wives.

DELILAH

Yes, and their wives. And they will hear my terms for saving them
from the disaster they are about to bring down upon themselves.
Do you understand? *(The MESSENGER shakes his head.)* You
don't have to. You are only a messenger boy. Take the message.
And I suggest you hurry. I won't wait long.
(MESSENGER looks at her for a moment, then realizes she is not
bluffing. He hastily packs up his attache case and exits.)

TERINAH

(Quietly curious.) You didn't tell them about his hair.

DELILAH

They never asked me. As soon as I said he was helpless, they rushed in, took him, and left without a word to me, without a glance. I don't think they even noticed I'd cut his hair. Or they thought it was some bit of love play between us. I thought they were going to kill him. So I didn't bother to say anything. You were the only person who asked me how I did it.

TERINAH

Are you really going to tell them? Don't. Delilah, don't tell them! *(Turns to audience.)* She can't, don't let her. Not after the way they treated her. You wouldn't, would you? *(Back to DELILAH.)* Let them have their trial, their spectacle. And let it happen...when blind Samson, with his hair grown back, carefully combed for the occasion, blind Samson, led in by his guards...and then...oh, I'd like to see it. But I won't. By that time, with this money, we'll be far from here, in a new life, with hardly a memory. Only later, after a long time, will come the news, the sweet news, that all...all were destroyed. All. Samson, the Philistines, all.

DELILAH

I am tempted.

TERINAH

Tempted? How can you hesitate?

DELILAH

I'd like to see them all coming here again, sober again, with that fear in their eyes again. Only, this time, I wonder what fine words they would use to persuade me, what promises...oh, no, I don't think I can stand the sight of them again.

TERINAH

Right. Let's leave. Now. When they come, we'll be gone. That's the perfect revenge.

151

DELILAH

(Shaking off her vengeful mood.) No. No, I ought to tell them. Set conditions and tell them.

TERINAH

What conditions? We're leaving. What do you want from them, more money? I wouldn't push this thing too far, Delilah; you're dealing with men who are capable of. . .

DELILAH

No. No more money.

TERINAH

Then what? What are your terms?

DELILAH

I don't know. I. . . when I said that, I was only thinking of making them come here, humiliating them. I was angry. I wanted to see them beg. But. . . no, no, I don't care about that, I don't want that. I suppose my conditions will be *(Shrugs.)* that they take Samson out of prison. Let him live out what is left of his life in some. . . decent, quiet place. . . where they can keep his strength clipped, confined, safe.

TERINAH

Is that all?

DELILAH

That's all.

TERINAH

Why not kill him? You said you wanted a clean kill.

DELILAH

I have learned something since I said that.

152

TERINAH

What?

DELILAH

That there is no such thing as a clean kill.

TERINAH

What is that supposed to mean! Learned something? You haven't
learned anything. *(To audience.)* Do you understand it? Those are
her terms? Instead of letting these bastards get what they deserve.
And him too, Samson! All of them, all together. Delilah, can't you
see the justice of it?

DELILAH

I don't want to talk about it anymore. I'm sick of the whole thing.
Come. Let's start packing our things while we wait.

TERINAH

We don't need to pack anything. We have plenty of money. We can
leave everything and just go, now.
(DELILAH shakes her head.)
You're really going to tell them. But why?

DELILAH

I don't want any more killing. I should never have gotten mixed up
in this. My first instinct was right. I should have refused them when
they came. Now I want to be through with them, once and for all.
But I don't want any more killing.

TERINAH

They'll only lie to you again. They'll accept your terms, but as soon
as we're gone, they'll kill him.

DELILAH

Yes, they probably will. But I will have done what I could. Even if
they kill him, I will have saved some lives. Many lives.

TERINAH

And you want to save their lives?

DELILAH

I don't want to be responsible for their deaths.
(TERINAH gives up, makes a gesture of hopelessness to under-stand. The MESSENGER has entered, hurriedly, upset, without attache case.)

DELILAH

You're alone?

MESSENGER

(Nods, breathing heavily, as if out of breath.)

DELILAH

You told them. . .

MESSENGER

Exactly what you said.

DELILAH

And they. . .

MESSENGER

They laughed. They called it. . . the trick. . .

TERINAH

The trick of a whore! *(She laughs.)*

MESSENGER

I told them you were sincere. That you really know something, that we are not safe yet. But they didn't believe me. They thought you wanted more money. They said they wouldn't be blackmailed by. . .

TERINAH

By a whore! *(She is laughing with furious delight.)*

MESSENGER

And that I was to tell you that if you were not gone from here before sunrise, you would be arrested. I did not dare to say anymore. They were beginning to look strangely at me. In a moment, I think I might have been arrested. I don't know. What shall I do? I tried, I...

DELILAH

You believe me.

MESSENGER

Yes, ma'am.

DELILAH

(More to herself than to him.) But they won't listen to you.

MESSENGER

They're all still drunk. Like everyone else. Ever since they took him. Parties. Speeches. Parades. They won't listen. But wait... would you be willing to tell me this information? Then I could wait till some time when they might be more willing to listen. No, I suppose after this, you wouldn't...

TERINAH

How can you even ask? If you think she would...

DELILAH

(Waves at her to be quiet.) Tell me. The trial. You are sure all the people will attend. Not just the generals and their people.

MESSENGER

Everyone will be there. Of course, the front seats will be reserved for important people, but there will be plenty of room in the upper tiers...

DELILAH

Well, that settles it, his strength is in...

TERINAH

Don't, Delilah! Don't tell him!

DELILAH

But, Terinah, all the people will be there, not just the generals. If I thought it would be only the generals, I might be tempted...to free all the people by letting...

TERINAH

Let them all die.

DELILAH

I can't. Some are innocent, some...

TERINAH

I was innocent! I was innocent when they destroyed my home, my family. Did any of the people help me then? I was half-dead when you took me in. They would have let me starve. They turned away from me as if I carried a plague, worse, as if I didn't even exist. You can't...

DELILAH

I can't be like them.

TERINAH

Delilah! *(She jumps up, but DELILAH is already speaking her next line.)*

DELILAH

It's his hair. His strength will grow back with it. Keep him shorn. *(TERINAH drops back into seated position, with a heavy sigh.)*

MESSENGER

Is that all?

DELILAH

Does that sound too fanciful? Now perhaps you don't believe me.

MESSENGER

I believe you. But I don't think they will.

DELILAH

The generals.

MESSENGER

Yes. And all that hair. It always was a mark of his defiance. I know they'll want him to look . . . hairy, wild, beastly, for the trial.

DELILAH

Then go directly to the people. Tell the people.

MESSENGER

They may be even less likely to believe. You have seen their mindless relief. They want to believe that finally they have peace. Safety. They want to forget their humiliation. They want to begin boasting again that we are the strongest of all nations, that we have never lost a war, that . . .

DELILAH

You must make them listen, make them realize that at this moment, when they feel safe again, when all that threatened them seems to be brought under control . . . that everything is about to collapse.
(MESSENGER looks uncomfortable, looks away.)

TERINAH

He's not going to say anything. He's afraid. He won't say a word!
(Her spirits are picking up.)

157

MESSENGER

I will! I will...report that the woman Delilah said...what you said. But in the present climate my message will be unpopular.

DELILAH

So, you will quote my words, and if they laugh...you will laugh with them and say no more.

MESSENGER

That is correct.

DELILAH

And the trial. Will you yourself stay away from the trial?

MESSENGER

(Hesitates.) It...it is my job to be there. I must...

TERINAH

(To audience.) The fool cannot even save himself!

MESSENGER

(At first to TERINAH, then gradually to audience, for the first time.) But what else can I do? Do you think I haven't always known something like this would come? Had to come? If not Samson, someone else, something else, created out of what we've done, what we've become. Yes, I live in a dying society. But I am a part of it, shaped by it. I doubt I could adjust to a better society, should a better one replace this one. Which is not at all certain. So I will die with this one. But...knowing destruction is near, I'm free, free to be a poet again. I will write what this woman did, how she vanquished Samson, how the generals used her and betrayed her, and how, in spite of them, she tried to save us all from the coming catastrophe. *(To DELILAH, with some enthusiasm.)* You will go down in history as a great hero. I will start now, while there is still time. Now. *(Exits hastily.)*

TERINAH

Judging by that little sample, I'd say he's a lousy writer.
(They look at each other and laugh.)
So, history will vindicate you, Delilah. Now are you satisfied?

DELILAH

(Smiles, shrugs.) Whatever he writes will be buried in the rubble.
Then the Hebrews will write their version of Samson's story. In that
version, he will be the innocent hand of God's vengeance, and I will
be a lying, avaricious seducer; at best a tool for fulfilling the words
of their prophets. Truth may be written by poets, but history is written by the victors. And it looks like the Hebrews are going to win
this one.

TERINAH

Whichever side wins, it makes no difference to us. Now are you
ready to go?

DELILAH

Go where?

TERINAH

Away from the land of the Philistines.

DELILAH

Where?

TERINAH

(Impatiently.) It doesn't matter where. Any place where there are
no Philistines.

DELILAH

And where might that be? Oh, Terinah. And you called *me* naive!
(They laugh, join hands, and exit.)

BEING A WRITER

I chose the title of this section carefully. It is not about writing, whose arduous joys I discussed in *Writing a Novel,* a book directed at people who want to write. Most people who say they want to write really mean that they want to "be a writer," which they imagine means to live a rich, respected, and glamorous life. The essays in this section should help to unmake that myth.

The first one, published in *California Living* in 1981, sets the proper tone, I think, for discussion of problems which are serious, but not the most serious in the world.

How to Talk to a Writer

For many years I was the only person I knew who was writing. At social gatherings I posed as a teacher (which I was). Then my first novel was published, blowing my cover. At the same time it seemed that everyone else had started writing too. For the next ten years I watched nonwriters becoming an endangered species, making abortive efforts to converse with these prickly, defensive, ubiquitous creatures—writers.

In sympathy with their struggle to achieve conversations which do not lapse into cold silence, sarcastic attack, or open violence, I offer a few rules for talking to a person introduced as "a writer."

(1) Do not ask if she has been published. If she hasn't, you will have scratched a raw nerve, vibrating with all the bitterness of her life. If she has been published, you will have revealed that, despite publication, you never heard of her, thereby scratching another, even more irritable nerve.

(2) If the writer is introduced to you as "Joe Bleau, author of the novel *Blackberry Nowhere*," do not ask him, "What is your novel about?" He spent four years and seven months writing his novel. He will consider your question an implication that all his efforts could just as easily be summed up in a few words.

Of course, if he has been introduced to you as "Joe Bleau, who wrote a book about osteoporosis," it is all right to ask him about that subject. His research (and possibly his nonwriting profession) has made him an expert, perhaps even a fanatic who loves to give impromptu lectures.

(3) To deal with the author you never heard of, quickly pull out a piece of paper and a pencil. Then say, "I'm afraid I don't know your work. How do you spell your name? Give me the titles of your books." This implies serious interest, even intent to buy the books. Even if she says her books are as yet unpublished, you can answer that you want to be alert when they do come out, thus implying that her forlorn hope of publication is not in vain. Put the paper carefully in your pocket and change the subject. After the party you may throw all these scraps away.

(4) Do not ask questions about process—like, what are you working on now? Or, how do you discipline yourself to write every day? You may genuinely admire the effort to write, but your question sounds like an atheist asking a Catholic how he *really* feels about the Virgin Mary. To protect the creative process, writers observe inexplicable taboos like never discussing works in progress, and perform odd rituals that get them going each day. Your polite, anthropological interest in their obsessive behavior makes them feel ridiculous.

(5) On the other hand, it's perfectly all right to ask questions about the *business* of writing. Any question about publishers and agents will turn a writer into an erupting volcano of fury. This works best if you are stuck with two or more writers, who will then compete to prove who has been most abused by agents and publishers. Once set in motion, this talk can go on for hours. When you get bored, you may move away without anyone noticing your desertion.

(6) Current literature is not a forbidden topic, but it is risky. If you mention a best seller, the writer will be too full of envy to have read it. If you mention a writer whose work seems related to that of the writer you are talking to, chances are they don't like each

other's work or were once friends but had a falling out. You may name an author who is universally admired, only to see the writer's lip curl as her eyes flash a cold, silent glare at you. Take courage—insist on an explanation. Perhaps she will knock the idol off his pedestal and relieve you of the tedium of reading him because you believed you *ought* to admire his work.

Dead authors are safer. If you really love Willa Cather, you and a writer may retire to a quiet corner where you will forge a lifelong bond while wallowing together in her genius.

(7) If you actually have read the books of the author you meet at a party, and you really admire them, feel free to lay on the praise with a shovel. But do not mention that you waited weeks to get his book from the library. What seems to you a tribute to his popularity is to him only a reminder of his penury. Chances are that no matter how famous this writer is, he is still juggling jobs to make ends meet. His suddenly clenched jaw means he is restraining himself from demanding why you will spend the price of a book many times over in bars, coffee houses, restaurants and movie houses, then go to the library because you "cannot afford" a book, from which price he gets only ten percent, at most.

(8) Do not ask this admired author to read the manuscript of your brother-in-law's epic poem. This is a teaching function, which he does for money, when he has to. Even if you offer him money, he may refuse, because people who ask for criticism are usually really after publication, and when the writer doesn't get it for them, accuse him of plagiarism. As to direct questions about how to get something published, the writer is useless, being preoccupied with the struggle to get his own next book into print.

(9) If you are overawed to be in the presence of a writer whose reputation is rising, do not try to conquer your feelings by insulting her. To be told that she is overweight or cannot create credible male characters, by a perfect stranger, in public, is disconcerting and not likely to lead to a friendly chat. It is almost as bad as trying to establish an affinity with her by saying, "I'd like to write if only I had the time, maybe starting with a children's book." She has, at considerable sacrifice, *made* time to write, and a good children's book is the hardest to write.

(10) Do not ask a writer if one of his novels is autobiographical. First of all, the question implies that the book was created by the

material, not by the skill and sweat of the writer. Secondly, the question says that books mean less to you than gossip. Thirdly, it's none of your business.

(11) As you have no doubt gathered by now, most writers would rather talk about anything but writing: your recipe for chutney, batting averages in middle-league baseball, bonsai, brain allergies, motorcycle clubs, illegal immigrants, Fred Astaire movies. A stab in the dark is sure to strike an interest of the writer or one of your own, which is just as good, since a writer will be interested in your interest in anything.

In fact you could just talk about yourself. A writer is probably the only person at a party who is willing to sit and listen, as long as what you say comes out of your raw need, with no idea that, God forbid, anyone should write it. (People who believe their lives "would make a great book" are usually mistaken.) And the writer is a safe repository for your private agonies and joys. If she uses anything you tell her in a book, it will be so transformed that you won't recognize it.

To tell the truth, recognition is sweet, but I miss those parties of the old days before anyone knew I wrote books. In those days I was a quiet nobody who ended up in the corner with someone who just needed to talk. In those days people were to me like windows through which I viewed a rich landscape of the soul; today they are too often like fun-house mirrors, blinding me with a distorted reflection of myself.

* * *

I left out one of the most important rules for talking to a writer: do not mention reading that nasty review of his or her latest book. I am suspicious of people who ask (like a TV reporter at a disaster), "How do you feel about the attack on you in yesterday's paper?" They may be ignorant of how acutely painful bad reviews are, but I always suspect they get some kick out of watching another's pain.

I never mention a negative review unless the injured author brings up the subject. I often call or write to congratulate a writer-friend on receiving praise, but I never call to commiserate, no matter what nasty thing was printed. Silence is always kinder. Silence can mean I missed that issue of the paper or dismissed the review at a glance. Silence helps keep the incident in perspective; any mention of it opens the wound afresh.

If someone attacks me or my work in print, I never, never answer the attack, no matter how vicious and patently stupid. The more stupid it is, the more likely the writer will get satisfaction out of knowing that s/he has drawn blood. Besides, a writer defending herself against a bad review always sounds not authoritative or threatening but peevish.

Am I saying that spiteful people should freely embarrass writers without anyone's calling them to account? No. I think they should be answered, but not by their victims. I would go further and say that the person who really believes a writer has been maligned has an obligation to write at least a brief defense to the offending publication. (And yes, send a copy to the victim, for this is not empty commiseration, but support.)

The one letter I have included in this collection is an example. I wrote it in response to an especially smart-aleck attack on a writer whom I do not know personally and whose work bores me. As can be seen from the context of my letter, the reviewer was an admirer who had turned on his hero, writing a petty attack which I felt should not have been printed. I answered with what I hoped was a light but firm slap on the wrist. I reasoned that even if my letter was not printed (it wasn't) it might encourage the book editor to think twice before printing and, in effect, legitimizing such tasteless attacks on writers.

In reprinting this letter I have omitted names of both victim and culprit. Any reader who spends time trying to guess who is who reveals the malicious streak that spiteful reviews feed on.

September 20, 1982

Dear Book Editor:

I have never been a fan of A, but I must defend him against Mr. B's attack. I understand B's frustration. In 1966 he "set out to become the world's foremost authority" on an overhyped author whose reputation is now declining. Tough luck for any would-be critic. But in his furious shotgun expression of his disappointment, B unfairly wounds A and some innocent bystanders as well.

Starting with A's former teaching base, Buffalo, where B assumes it's "very difficult to be creative." That's the kind of smug remark San Franciscans make about places like Sacramento—B's base. I hasten to add that I never say things like that. I always assumed it was difficult to be creative anywhere.

"The end is near" for A's creativity, concludes B, after finding A's latest novel on a remainder table "less than a year" after publication. I wonder how many writers read that pronouncement with an aching heart, reminding themselves that their book's presence on a remainder table indicates nothing but slow sales, never an infallible sign of low quality, often just the opposite. Since B's blurb lists no books of his own, I assume he has no personal experience of the process of publication, which does not excuse his cruelty but could explain part of his attitude toward published writers.

Finally, although B claims to have been a mature reader as early as 1966, he must still be an adolescent. How else can we explain his final shot? "Perhaps A—turned 52 this year—should just shut down the machine and confine his future writing to marginal remarks on student fiction."

Sincerely,

Dorothy Bryant, turned 52 this year

* * *

Two months after I wrote that letter, I was accused of attacking Katherine Anne Porter in my review of her biography by Joan Givner (*San Francisco Chronicle,* November 14, 1982). Writers who had known Porter personally were "upset," though none said that Givner's unflattering portrait was false. One chided me for not utterly rejecting Givner's biography because it is weak on Porter's writing. I replied that there were piles of books on Porter's fiction, but nothing reliable on her life till Givner dug up the facts. Another writer said I had "redeemed" myself with the second half of the review, as if my opening summary of the unchallenged facts were a sin. A third writer suggested I should have rearranged my review to tone down the harsh opening. I doubt such a change would have placated Porter's friends, and it surely would have wrecked the review, which gets it full impact from the turn-around that comes at midpoint. Is it possible some people didn't read that far? I stand by it, as is. Given a 1000 word limit for a 500 page book, I made an unapologetic defense of one of my favorite writers and, by implication, a defense of all artists trying to survive in a world which, as Hemingway said, "eats its writers."

Joan Givner's
Katherine Anne Porter

Katherine Anne Porter was a liar. She lied about her origins, in-inventing a Southern belle's family in decline, complete with slaves-become-family-retainers, when the truth is she was born in a log cabin to a dirt-poor Texas family. She lied about her health, always "going to pieces" with illnesses that mysteriously disappeared when someone gave her money for a trip or released her from a teaching commitment. She lied about her role in historic events. Her brief meeting with Goering in the 1930s was inflated to acquaintance with Hitler and futile attempts to publish warnings against him. Actually she never met Hitler, and her writing (mostly letters) from that time is standard tourist stuff. She lied about her religion, her age, and even her name, furiously denying it when an innocent researcher uncovered her birth name: Callie Porter.

She lied about the reasons for her small output, citing the demands of earning a living and domestic responsibilities. Although she had little cash until she was seventy (when she made a bundle on her one novel, a mediocre piece of work) she rarely, after the age of thirty, held a job, never had children, and though a marvelous cook when she wanted to be, never really kept house for anyone. The truth was that she was housed and supported by husbands, friends, publishers, and admirers who hoped to create the conditions in which she could write more. That she didn't is attributable to Porter's forever rushing away from quiet working conditions toward some adventure—usually soap opera romances with men who became progressively younger than she.

She had a mean streak, which widened as she grew older, often turning on friends who had been most loyal and helpful. She was moralistic, harshly judging the foibles of others. The hint of anti-Semitism in her novel *Ship of Fools* was real, supported by remarks in her private letters. Toward the end of her life, she began making traditional racist and sexist remarks. In her last published work *The Never-Ending Wrong,* the self-aggrandizing mean streak is embarrassingly naked.

These facts are told with documentation and without malice by Joan Givner, who was chosen by Porter to write her biography, and who worked with complete cooperation of Porter's family. What are we to make of such a gap between the work and the life?

We could try denying the quality of the work, revising earlier evaluations. But that won't work. "Pale Horse, Pale Rider" remains one of the great novellas of American literature. How about the opposite view, that Porter's pretensions and cruelties were a necessary part of her talent—the artistic temperament from which great work flows? I can't buy that, having known too many pretentious and ruthless liars who never produced anything but misery for themselves and others.

We are left with that awful, perennial, and perhaps naive question: Doesn't the artist become a better person by reaching the truths expressed in great art? Well, maybe—maybe not. Maybe the old theologians were right: we are all sinners who, with variable frequency, perform acts which momentarily lift us above universal human error. This view, incidentally, is implicit in Porter's best fiction.

Putting such questions aside, let us examine Porter's life as the survival of an artist. By the age of forty, Porter was established as one of the best writers of her time. Yet she made only a few dollars from the sale of the stories that won her such acclaim. For the next thirty years her fame grew and grew; her income did not.

Fame and penury make a nasty combination; being fawned upon by rich people when you're not sure where next month's rent is coming from does not improve your character. Conning those people into lending you a house in Bermuda or moving in on your friends or scrambling for a grant to get you through the year or promising a publisher you'll work on what he wants (that big novel) so he'll keep feeding you advances or marrying for support—such means, though they seem easier than getting a job, exact a price.

Porter's Southern belle pretensions and her "fragile" health (she lived to age ninety) were deceptions that *worked* to get her time and money. Pay for work done was meager; pay for work *promised* increased along with honors as time passed without production. If Porter was a hypocrite, it was in response to a society which financially rewarded her hypocrisy, but not her talent.

Is it possible that her inner fury at the success of such manipulation broke out in anger, cruelty, prejudice, even in romantic flights from the work she loved? After all, her early work is strongly feminist, while her manipulative techniques were stereotypical "feminine wiles," surely a violation of deep instincts.

And more damaging to *us* than any of her lies was the violation of her talent by working off-and-on for twenty years on the "great American novel" demanded by publishers for economic success. It paid off as they promised, but it took time that could have gone into work better suited to her talents. By the time the payoff came, her best working years were gone.

Porter must have wanted us to know the truth after her death, else she would not have turned over such full documentation to so thorough an investigator. The question now is whether we will draw sound conclusions from that truth.

* * *

Like other human beings, writers sometimes suffer more serious problems than the pains of publication. When they do, the rest of society is lucky, because the writer can use his talent to articulate pain and identify abuse. Dean Lipton's experience of all too familiar frustration, abuse, and neglect was vividly detailed in his book *Malpractice*. My review of it appeared in the *San Francisco Review of Books* in 1978.

Dean Lipton's *Malpractice*

Early this year I spoke to a group of writers in San Francisco. As my eyes swept the room, they blinked at the sight of a man standing in the rear. His face was askew, half of it going off in a direction of its own, as if expressing a mad, sad split of personality. Afterward, the man approached me; his slightly blurred speech made me conclude that a stroke had shaken his handsome face. His name I recognized as that of a local writer and long-time director of the San Francisco Writers Workshop, but I could not recall reading any recent work of his.

Having read Dean Lipton's *Malpractice,* I now know that he did not suffer a stroke, and I understand why this book is the only one he has completed in the past ten years.

In 1967 Lipton awoke from minor ear surgery to find that the right side of his face had fallen. He was unable to close his right eye and virtually unable to speak. Doctors told him his face would return to normal in a few days. After a few days they said, a few weeks. They prescribed physical therapy, massage. As the months passed they became more silent, evasive, contemptuous, insulting, dismissive. "Well, after all, Mr. Lipton, you aren't a twenty-five-year-old girl." Somehow, between denials and evasions, Lipton learned that the surgeon had accidentally severed a facial nerve.

Lipton hired the best-known San Francisco firm of malpractice lawyers just before the statute of limitations on his case would have run out. After binding him to them with a contract giving them the customary half of whatever settlement he might get, they ignored his welfare much as his doctors had. They set the prayer (legalese for the amount of money sued for) too low. They forgot to advise him to have pictures taken before and after the numerous plastic surgeries which followed. (He has so far undergone twenty operations; the face I saw is his improved one.) They seemed bored with him and rather friendly with the opposition lawyers. Lipton fired them and hired two talented and conscientious young lawyers, who, bound by the first contract, eventually had to split their fee with the first firm.

Then there were the courts. Raising the prayer proved almost impossible. One attempt, Lipton suspects, failed because he had once criticized the presiding judge during a political campaign. The strategies, the delays, and the general air of indifference (familiar to anyone with even minor courtroom experience) were devastating to a man who already felt that his life had been destroyed.

It took six years to come to trial and to more refinements of the case. Not only was his disfigurement more difficult to assess legally than a lost arm or leg, but there was the troublesome fact of Lipton's being a writer. Courts measure settlements in terms of what the victim would be likely to earn throughout his life if not impaired by the malpractice. Lipton had not made much money up to the time of his injury. He might never make much, or he could tumble into bestsellerdom and make millions. Regardless of income, what happens to that intangible, the creative energy of a handsome, admittedly vain, outgoing, intense writer, lecturer, teacher, administrator of political campaigns and journalist who is suddenly rendered visually repulsive and inarticulate? Suffering invaluable losses, the plaintiff is forced to make his demands for justice in terms of money and to watch his life being weighed in court in terms of money.

Lipton sensed a deeper problem in his being a writer, a prejudice against him in court. It seemed that his lawyers' attempts to show the special damage to him as an artist evoked the mixture of contempt and envy which artists often encounter, at least in this country—a complex attitude which he might have explored in more depth.

Another complex question was the nature of the malpractice: was it the initial accident or the succeeding denials, insults, and the delays in trying remedies like nerve transplant? In this medical Watergate, the more destructive and far-reaching acts were felt by Lipton to be part of the cover-up, rather than the original crime. Indeed, considering his experience, Lipton is not hard on ineffectual doctors. He expresses a special fondness for one follow-up surgeon who blurted in honest exasperation, "Mr. Lipton, I haven't done you any good at all!"

173

Throughout the trial, the surgeon who maimed him insisted on referring to the results as a "facial weakness." But Lipton's face was in court to contradict him, and some doctors with the courage and stature to break silence took Lipton's side. The jury awarded him $500,000. Even this was threatened by an unsympathetic judge. (Judges have the power to reduce settlements awarded by juries.) After fees and expenses Lipton ended up with $188,000 and considerable knowledge of the "sheer human callousness" of too many medical and legal professionals.

It might be said that a weakness of the book is Lipton's tendency to harangue the reader. I can imagine him in his own writers' workshop, pointing out that some conclusions may be more effectively left to the reader, that some angry accusations need not be repeated. He might even suggest some techniques for more effectively individualizing characters; after a while one has trouble keeping track of all those doctors.

But—I guess—so did he, during this past decade of surgery, infections, side effects, psychiatric probings, and pre-dawn sleepless hours of loneliness, rage, and despair. Perhaps the "faults" of the book best illuminate the agony he suffered as a victim of malpractice in the broadest sense—the faults and abuses of our medical and legal systems. The strengths of the book show a strong revival of the creative powers so gravely injured.

* * *

Shortly after reviewing Dean Lipton's book, I became aware of another writer in court, this time in a case which came directly out of her writing. I noticed some brief and confusing references in the newspapers to a case of libel against a novelist, a case she lost, then lost again in the California Appeals Court. My curiosity aroused, I went to the University of California's Boalt Hall Library, where publication of appeals court opinions are available to all. I studied the appeals court opinion. I read *Touching,* the novel by Gwen Davis which was supposed to have libeled a psychotherapist named Bindrim. I read whatever articles I could find about the case. I contacted the author by phone, and began to talk to her and to others about the case.

The more I read and talked, the more appalled I was, not only by the court action but by the response of people, including writers. I never met anyone who had read the appeals court opinion or the novel itself, but everyone I met had opinions, which nearly always leaned in favor of the plaintiff and against the novelist. When I brought up the points detailed in the following article, people looked bored—and, indeed, the intricacies of libel law can be boring unless you are being sued. The consensus among people I nagged was that a minor Hollywood writer had made a lot of money on a dirty book which broke confidentiality of a group therapist and his clients, and she was not worth fighting for. Given a more respectable case, they would, of course, come to the defense of free speech, etc., etc. Outside of legal journals, the only informed article I ran across was one written by Nat Hentoff. The only writer I knew personally who did not equivocate was Kay Boyle, who cancelled her contract with Davis's publisher (for reasons made clear by my article.)

I sent query letters to over a dozen national magazines selected for their concern for First Amendment rights. All but one refused to look at my article. That one kept it for two months. When I telephoned, an editor said she had decided to have a staff person write up the case. (I accused her of planning to pirate my research—by this time I was feeling almost as persecuted as the defendant in the case.) Two liberal magazines which had refused to read my article published statements by the plaintiff or by his lawyer. I wrote letters to counter their statements with facts from the court proceedings; my letters were neither printed nor answered.

My article finally appeared in the *San Francisco Bay Guardian* in May 1980. It remains, I believe, the only summary in laymen's language of what actually happened in the case of *Bindrim versus Davis and Doubleday.*

175

The New Censorship

Let's get the facts of the case straight first. In 1969 Gwen Davis, Los Angeles author of ten novels, attended a weekend nude encounter group therapy session led by psychologist Paul Bindrim. She signed a contract not to take pictures or write articles about the session. Two months later, she signed a contract with Doubleday for a novel whose setting is a nude encounter session, and in 1971 the novel *Touching* was published. Bindrim wrote to Doubleday protesting the implied criticism of the therapy techniques described in the novel and demanded that they cease publication. After consultation with Davis, Doubleday concluded that the fictional therapist did not resemble Bindrim and that the other aspects of his complaint, criticism of a profession, are protected by the First Amendment. Doubleday then sold paperback rights to New American Library.

Bindrim sued Davis and Doubleday for libel in Los Angeles Superior Court. He won a judgment of $50,000 against Davis and $25,000 against Doubleday. A move for a new trial was blocked by the judge's offer that no new trial would be granted if Bindrim would take half of the settlement. He accepted. Davis and Doubleday went to California Appeals Court, which not only upheld the original judgment but increased the penalty against Doubleday, on the grounds of "greater wealth." The California Supreme Court refused to review the case. Finally, in December 1979, the United States Supreme Court refused to review it. This case then becomes precedent, law in California. Doubleday is now suing author Davis for $138,000 in penalties and costs, citing the "hold harmless" clause of their contract, in which the author assumes responsibility for possible libel or other charges.

Touching tells the story of Soralee, who attends a weekend nude encounter session, gains insight despite her antipathy toward the psychiatrist leading it, but dies in an auto accident on her way home, partly caused by her being dangerously "high" from the intensive treatment. In two passages within the approximately 70,000-word novel, the psychiatrist, Dr. Herford, uses words that became central to the libel suit. When a woman hesitates to unwrap her towel at the beginning of the session, he says, "Drop it, bitch." Later he urges a minister who is having trouble getting his wife to come to a nude encounter to "grab her by the cunt" and get her there.

Touching was the kind of novel Doubleday could promote easily in order to capitalize on a titillating trend. But it also contained some serious criticism of the group therapy sessions that were coming into full fashion at the time it was published, and especially of irresponsible self-appointed gurus who gathered together admittedly troubled people in order to crack open their structures of containment and make them spill their "real" selves. A dangerous business.

At all court levels, rulings supported Davis's writing about the group she attended. No therapist can treat a patient and then swear her to secrecy about the treatment. The contract Davis signed was worthless, and her attempt to comply with it is what got her into trouble. As one judge said, if Davis had reported everything just as she saw it, then stated her opinion that Bindrim was irresponsible, crooked, or worse, she would have been safe. Opinion is not libel.

What is libel? The California Civil Code defines libel as "a false and unprivileged publication which exposes any person to hatred, contempt, ridicule or obloquy or which causes him to be shunned or avoided or which has a tendency to injure him in reputation."

The troublesome word in this case is "false." A work of fiction is by definition not factual. How can it be libelous if it declares itself to be nonfactual? Bindrim charged that although the novel purported to be fiction, it was so close to the therapy techniques he used that, despite the difference in name, age, appearance, and credentials, he was recognizable. He produced three witnesses (one a fellow psychologist) who had attended his therapy sessions and said they recognized him in the book from the therapy style.

Then Bindrim gave libel law a special twist by declaring himself a "public figure." Under libel law a public figure, who may expect to find his or her name frequently in print, has no grounds for suit unless he or she can prove "actual malice" on the part of the writer making false statements. Supposedly, as a "public figure," Bindrim would have to make an even stronger case. Actually, in the words of dissenting Appeals Court Judge Files, Bindrim's public figure status was ". . . a tactic to enhance his argument that any unflattering portrayal of his kind of therapy defames him."

And how did he prove actual malice? Bindrim brought complete tape recordings to show parallels between the novel and the session

Davis attended. Malice, he charged, lay in the "false" incidents, like the death of Soralee, and more particularly in the "vulgar" language used by the fictional therapist.

How's that again? Davis wrote a work she called fiction. Bindrim stepped forward to claim the identity of a fictional character, offering tapes to show parallels between fiction and fact, asserting that the fictional parts of the book were malicious, libelous, because they were false—that is, fiction. Again quoting dissenting Judge Files; "When the publication purports to be fiction, it is absurd to infer malice because the fiction is false."

The death of Soralee in the novel (Bindrim's tapes exactly paralleled the fictional therapist's futile warning about being "high... so drive carefully") could be construed as critical of the therapy technique, but such criticism is definitely protected by the First Amendment. Everything came down finally to those "vulgar" words.

The defense asked Superior Court Judge Wells to instruct the jury to that effect, showing all the parts of the book that were constitutionally protected and pointing out that the few instances of "vulgar" words must carry the whole weight of the libel charges. The defense also asked Judge Wells to brief the jury on precedent regarding "public figure" libel, which states that a large segment of the public called "the average reader" must recognize Bindrim as the character in the book.

Judge Wells did no such thing. He told the jury to consider the novel "as a whole," not pointing out which implied criticisms were constitutionally protected. Then he did something truly mind-boggling. Not only did he refuse the defense's instruction regarding "the average reader," he went on to interpret libel law in such a way that the jury could do nothing but give a verdict against the defendants.

In a twist that rivaled Bindrim's "public figure" ploy, Judge Wells reached for a section of the law that states that telling a damaging lie to only one person constitutes "publication" of libel, a definition that has nothing to do with with books or newspapers. Then he instructed the jury that Bindrim need only prove that "a third person read the statement and reasonably understood the defamatory meaning and that the statement applied to plaintiff." In other words, Bindrim could have left two of his witnesses at home. According to this crude patchwork of law, he needed only one person to say he or she had read the book, recognized Bindrim, and thought he had been defamed.

How could anything so absurd be upheld by the Court of Appeals? I have read the majority opinion expressed by Judges Kingsley and Jefferson over and over. They support Wells's juxtaposition of misfit points of libel law, and they condemn fiction because it is not factual. And they keep coming back to the use of "crude and vulgar" words "of the rankest sort," especially the word "cunt." Kingsley, showing the parallels between the novel and the tape recordings, quotes just that passage from the novel and only that passage, placing it beside the tape transcript to prove that Bindrim never said that word. (Bindrim's lawyer quoted the same passage in a recent article in *The Nation,* implying that it was typical of dozens of examples introduced in court. It is not, and most of the other examples of "false" passages are implied criticism of therapy that fall under First Amendment protection.) Dismissing this First Amendment right to criticize a therapy technique, Judge Jefferson wrote that Davis would have been safe had she "limited her novel to a truthful or fictional description of the techniques employed in nude encounter therapy." I quote that phrase because I have read it enough times to memorize it, and I still don't understand it.

Though I don't understand it, I believe it hints at an ambivalence, even hostility, toward writers. I am reminded of the recently published *Malpractice* by Dean Lipton, which describes his suit against a surgeon who horribly disfigured his face. Lipton found that when it came to placing a value on his life work, writing, impaired if not destroyed by the slip of a scalpel, even his own lawyers tended to deny its worth, and after the jury had awarded him damages, the judge arbitrarily reduced the amount to little more than what Bindrim got for "proving" that vulgar word attributed to him.

Writers are familiar with this attitude, expressed in its most benign form as "There's a book I'd like to write too, if I only had the time." In other words, writing is not work, it is a self-indulgent pastime requiring no special talent, skill, or training.

When the writer is a woman, there are added prejudices. If she creates unsympathetic male characters and puts into their mouths "vulgar" words traditionally reserved for the use of men, she will encounter special hostility. And if she, like Gwen Davis, gets a $150,000 advance for doing it (Judge Kingsley considered the amount important enough to write it into his opinion), she may arouse a peculiar mixture of deep-lying prejudices.

These are not just idle speculations. Davis (whom I did not know personally) told me that at one point during her ordeal, a Doubleday lawyer testified that Doubleday went ahead with publication because Davis assured them that the book was fiction. Whereupon one of the judges replied, "You mean in a country where, daily, citizens who are above reproach commit crimes, you took the word of a *writer*?"

There is even firmer evidence of prejudice against Davis in a peculiar error written into the appeals court action. Again and again Judge Kingsley refers to "tape recordings the author had taken of the actual sessions." He cites the author's possession of tapes as proof of the "actual malice" that is a necessary component to prove libel, since Davis showed a "reckless disregard for the truth" as recorded on her own tapes, available to her while she was writing the book.

But Davis had no tapes. The tapes were Bindrim's, introduced as evidence by him. Since the appeals court erroneously cited ownership of tapes as evidence of "actual malice" by Davis, her attorneys asked for a rehearing. Their motion was denied.

The case raises interesting questions about the relation between author and publisher. Doubleday's "greater wealth" is, it seems, to be protected and maintained at the expense of its authors. There is something ugly about a huge corporation throwing its legal weight behind an author while planning to sock her with the cost if it loses. Doubleday's suit against Davis dramatizes the irresponsible stance of a publisher who contracts to print, promote, and distribute a book while writing into the contract a refusal to stand behind the content of the book. If anything good comes out of this case, it may be the rising protest of authors against the "hold harmless" clause in all contracts.

Yet, since losing the support of her publisher, Davis has lost some of her support from fellow writers. *The American Lawyer* dredged up the fact that nearly twenty years ago Davis herself got an $8,000 out-of-court settlement by threatening to sue Ken Kesey for using her as a model for a character in *One Flew Over the Cuckoo's Nest,* and that she evidently did so in revenge for Kesey's having threatened to sue her over characters resembling him and his wife in Davis's first novel.

But if distaste for such antics causes people to lose sight of the real issues and to withdraw support from Davis, we are all of us, writers and readers, in for bad times. Maybe we are anyway.

The dissenting opinion of Judge Files of the California Appeals Court brings us back to the real issues. "The effect is to mulct the defendants for the exercise of their First Amendment rights..." by a decision which "...poses a grave threat to any future work of fiction which explores the effect of techniques claimed to have curative value."

The threat is even broader. Consider the recent suits by groups like Synanon and Church of Scientology, who threaten suits against writing that carries even the breath of criticism of any of their practices and policies—curative, financial, or otherwise.

Then consider the most frightening case of all. Remember that the United States Supreme Court which refused to review the Davis case is the same court which just upheld the CIA suit against Frank Snepp. Snepp must now pay to the government all income from his book *Decent Interval,* written in defiance of a contract of confidentiality signed while Snepp was employed by the CIA, a contract which required CIA approval of anything he wrote about the agency, and obviously a contract with far wider implications than the Bindrim-Davis contract so quickly and unanimously thrown out of court. This is the same court that is so provocatively portrayed in the book *The Brethren* and, quite possibly, since publication of that book, not feeling very friendly toward *any* writers.

From now on will publishers submit manuscripts for government approval of political material before they chance publication? From now on will publishers reject any book that might offend a well-heeled and litigious organization? From now on will serious writers of fiction be able to write at all, knowing their attempts to disguise material taken from life may be judged libelous, leaving them open to the vengeance and greed of anyone who can show up in court with *one* witness to back his accusations?

The new censorship will be self-censorship, in an effort to stay out of the courts that are making it clear to us where they stand on writers and the First Amendment.

* * *

I attempted to add some notes on the aftermath of this case but gave up. After stating that Doubleday and Davis settled out of court and that some publishers now provide libel insurance for their authors, I would have had to list a mass of suits, threats to sue, and out-of-court settlements. This epidemic of litigation, most of it now aimed at nonfiction reporting, could be covered only by another lengthy article, followed by ceaseless updating. Even such an article would be limited to summarizing documented threats. There is no way of knowing how many reports are being killed, how many books rejected by publishers, how many not attempted at all, through fear of the expense of even successfully defending a libel suit.

* * *

Different writers respond in different ways to the problems of being a writer. My way of coping with some of the problems is to follow the old tradition of self-publishing. In 1978 I was asked to write a detailed history of how and why I chose this way. It was published in *Frontiers* (University of Colorado). What follows is an updated version of that article.

My Publisher/Myself

When I started writing in 1960, I expected to put in ten years of daily work before producing something worthy of publication. By 1970 I was a little ahead of schedule. I had an M.A. in creative writing with an honorable mention in the 1964 Joseph Henry Jackson Awards for my thesis novel. I had published one short story in a little magazine and was contributing monthly articles to *Freedom News,* one of the many Bay Area underground papers of the sixties. I had written the first novel I thought worth publishing, *Ella Price's Journal,* which a New York agent had been trying to sell for two years. And I had just finished *The Comforter,* a mystical fantasy which I sent off to my agent. After several months of silence, I wrote to ask him about his progress with either novel. He replied that my second novel was so bad he would never show it to publishers for fear of prejudicing them against me.

I knew he was wrong, but what could I do, fire him? Then I'd be even worse off. As an unpublished novelist I'd had a hard enough time getting him. I remember holding his letter in my hand, shaking it at my husband Bob, and letting my anger pour out. "Do you know how many writers have published their own books?" I shouted. "Virginia Woolf! Thoreau! D. H. Lawrence! Upton Sinclair!" I didn't mention Dostoevsky and Mark Twain because at the time I didn't know that at the height of their fame, each had gone back to self-publishing. "Blake! Shelley! Whitman!"

"O.K.," Bob said. "Let's do it."

We went to our friends out of whose basement came the *Freedom News* and hired their typesetter to do *The Comforter* on their justowriter, a cranky machine which justifies margins and prints a serviceable, newspaperlike type. We got quotes from printers. Bob studied and drew dozens of butterflies trying to perfect one for the cover. At each stage there were new problems, new decisions I felt unprepared to deal with: page size, cover design, title pages, location of page numbers. Had I ever *looked* at all those books I'd read? In all those years of reading, writing, and juggling abstract ideas in the classroom, had I lost the ability to make something real? At the worst times it was Bob who quietly asked the right questions, learning what we needed to know to go on step by step to completion.

Eventually we had 3,000 paperback books, produced at a cost of $1,800. We priced the book at $1.95. With forty percent to bookstores, twelve percent more to distributors (if we could even get them to take it), printing costs of sixty cents per book, postage, wrapping, invoices, and gas for delivery, we might clear twenty cents per book. Out of this twenty cents would come any promotion we did, not to mention wages for us as publishers or royalties for me as author. Obviously we would be lucky to break even. But we had been warned by a bookseller friend that no one would spend more than $2, if that, for a novel by an unknown. People didn't buy novels much, anyway. "Now if you could write a how-to book...." The important thing, we had decided, was to get me in print. We tried to think of that $1,800 as spent for fun, as some unpublished authors take a trip to console themselves for not being in print. And, of course, we had hopes.

Our naivete was reflected in the cover we designed: a single black butterfly on a white background. No title; that was on the back cover. The design had seemed logical, even clever: since we couldn't afford a splashy, colorful cover, we would have one that was not only thematically correct, but also intriguing. I imagined a browser in a bookstore seeing the simple black butterfly on the untitled cover of the book lying on a table, picking up the book and... presto, hooked! It never occurred to me to ask how I was going to get the book into a bookstore, let alone in one of the coveted spaces on those tables.

At the first bookstore I approached, I got a complete course in the problems of distributing self-published work, delivered at the top of the manager's voice. "I never heard of you! Has this thing been reviewed? We don't stock vanity press! You didn't put the title on the spine? There's no demand for novels! I don't even have room for the books I *want* to stock! Don't bother me, I'm busy!" My treatment at a couple of other stores in Berkeley was less brutal, but essentially the same. Fiction would not be stocked unless reviews had created a demand for it; newspapers and magazines reviewed only hard-bound books put out by major New York publishers.

With a mixture of bravado and despair, we began giving books away. We got one review—in *Freedom News*. And we got further glimmers of our ignorance. I'd copyrighted *The Comforter* but hadn't registered with the Library of Congress or with *Books in Print* or...it seemed there were so many things about publishing I hadn't thought of.

Then came word from my agent. Lippincott was mildly interested in *Ella Price's Journal*. An editor suggested some good changes. I made the changes, Lippincott took the book, and we celebrated (I didn't cry when I heard the news; Bob did). It was all over. I now had My Publisher.

At San Francisco State University, back in the early sixties, I had been told that a publisher takes a first novel not expecting great sales, but hoping to develop that writer, so that by the eighth or tenth novel—when the writer's reputation is assured—the publisher has a solid, money-making backlist of her work. Even while that was being said to me, it was no longer true. But I still believed it, and I told Bob, "Let's get rid of these boxes of books, give them all away, donate them to schools or prisons or something."

He was quiet for a moment, then shook his head. "Not yet."

Ella Price's Journal came out in fall 1972 to complete silence: no promotion, nothing but a few local reviews, and in a hard-cover edition costing more than the main audience for a "re-entry woman's novel" would pay. The first printing of 5,000 was enough for the market.

Sinclair Lewis said that whenever he heard of a good new novel, he waited two years. Then if it was still around, he read it. That test of quality would not work today, for the best as well as the worst has little chance of being around that long. Most serious novels, if they ever do get into print, are published in an act analogous to dropping the book off the edge of a cliff into a chasm, never to be seen again. Nearly 40,000 books are published each year in this country. Without big money promotion, few will even get into the crowded bookstores, which return slow sellers to the publishers after a few weeks. At the end of a year or two, slow sellers are cleared out of the warehouse and end up on bargain tables, called remainders. Then they disappear.

But I had a lucky break. My agent sold *Ella* to *Redbook,* which condensed it and received about twenty times the usual reader mail in response to it. It was this response that made Signet buy it to reprint it as a cheap, mass-market paperback. I looked forward eagerly to the appearance of the paperback, scheduled for fall 1973 and certain, I thought, to reach its larger audience—all those women all over the country represented by the *Redbook* response.

Then the Signet edition appeared, with a cover featuring a sulky woman in a negligee, with pallid flowers and jacket copy which not only falsified the book, but carefully hid the fact that it had anything to do with returning to school or with the inner search of journal writing. Furious, I wrote to Signet that the audience for the book would never touch it. Their reply? They might consider changing the cover if the book went into a second printing. However, if it sold enough to go into another printing, they would only prove that there was nothing wrong with the original cover.

Ella sold in college bookstores, where it was ordered by teachers who knew what was inside the cover. It hardly sold at all in the drugstores and supermarkets, where I had hoped it would reach those isolated women who had written those agonized letters to *Redbook.* After a few weeks on the supermarket rack, the distributor takes back the unsold books, tears off the front cover and sends it to the publisher for a refund. Then he destroys the books. About 60,000 *Ella's* met that fate; 40,000 sold. Three years later, despite disappointing sales, Signet reprinted *Ella* with a new cover. It sold steadily, but too slowly for the slim paperback profit margin. Signet dropped *Ella* in 1979.

Meanwhile, I had suffered a worse setback. In 1972, upon publication of *Ella Price's Journal,* my agent sent *The Comforter* to Lippincott, which promptly rejected it, just as confused as my agent that the author of *Ella* would come up with something so different. "That's all right," said my agent. "I just gave them that weird one to break the option clause. Now we'll hit them with your third." For, of course, I had kept on writing and had finished *Miss Giardino,* which my agent was sure Lippincott would find irresistible. But the editor who had loved Ella said of Miss Giardino, "I can't identify with that woman." And that was that.

By now I was beginning to see how publishing had changed since the days when a publisher "developed" an author. Publishing companies had merged and had been bought out by conglomerates for whom a book was just another product, like corn flakes: to be processed, packaged, and sold quickly. In fact, books had a shorter shelf life than foods pumped full of preservatives. Certain serious novelists continued to be published, if they had a firm place in the literary market or the mass market or the academic market. But if you weren't in one of those categories with those chosen few, each of your books had to make it on its own, make it big, and make it fast. "It was a miracle," my agent said, "that we got *Ella* published." He promised to keep trying, but I guess he lost heart, because soon I was hearing nothing from him. And when I went on writing, sending him my fourth and fifth novels, he didn't even read them.

Back to *The Comforter,* which in 1973 was beginning to sell. Some of the friends to whom I'd given copies were teachers, and, finding that this seemingly simple dream fantasy stimulated heated discussion and strong emotional response, they began to use it in high school and college classes. Other changes were happening. Women's bookstores were opening, and the great mother of them all, Woman's Place in Oakland, discovered *The Comforter* and began pushing it as a feminist utopian novel. But some changes didn't help me after all. Distributors open to small press books were started. I applied to two; both refused to distribute *The Comforter.*

But in addition to school sales and women's bookstore sales, we were getting orders for single copies from New Hampshire or New Zealand, usually accompanied by loving notes telling how the person had stumbled on the book or had been given it as a gift and now wanted to buy two or three to give away. A Jungian analyst came to me and bought 100 to give to patients and colleagues. By 1975 we had almost sold out our 3,000, with no reviews, no promotion, no entry to more than a few bookstores. I wrote to ten mass paperback houses which publish fantasy, quoting figures, offering the book. Two replied. They said no. By now it was clear that my position as a writer would remain precarious—both in terms of publication and money—for a long time, probably all my life.

I had been teaching since the age of sixteen, but from the time I started writing, I'd had trouble mixing writing and teaching; they drew from the same energy source. Now I was forty-five years old, and my position as a teacher was the one secure, lucrative, respected thing I had going for me.

So I turned in my resignation. It was another act of defiance like the decision to self-publish, one I don't recommend unless the writer has a working spouse.

"Good," said Bob. "Now, we'd better think about reprinting *The Comforter*."

But before we could, I was visited by Anne Kent Rush of Moon Banks, co-publishing with Random House. She wanted to publish *The Comforter* as one of four on her first list in fall 1976. Under this co-publishing agreement, she explained, I would receive the close attention and cooperation of Moon Books, with the financing, promotion, and distribution benefits of Random House. I fired my agent (who had stopped answering my letters and always hated *The Comforter* anyway) and signed a contract no different from the one he had negotiated for my first novel. Rush supported my request that the book be published simultaneously in hard- and soft-cover, so that the market already established would not be lost by an expensive hard-cover book. She consulted me at all stages of production. I approved the cover, the typeface, the general design, and when she said *The Comforter* sounded like a quilt, I chose a new title, the last line of the book, *The Kin of Ata Are Waiting For You*.

Again Bob and I celebrated. I finally had My Publisher.

Not quite. Moon Books published "feminist material." So I was still not being published as an *author* to be developed. Each book was to be considered separately. Anne Kent Rush was dubious about my other work fitting the Moon Books definition of feminist; nevertheless, in 1977, she took *Miss Giardino* to Random House for co-publishing. Random rejected it. So the final decisions were still being made in New York by the same people who had been rejecting my work for years. A second miracle had occurred, but no natural laws had altered.

Speaking of New York, what was happening with the great promotion resources of Random House? There were no excerpts in fantasy magazines, no contracts with science fiction book clubs. In fact, there were no reviews. Even my first novel had received reviews in little papers in Kansas or Texas, so I knew review copies had gone out. This time I wondered. But I was undaunted, having learned that most novelists will get no media attention other than what they can generate for themselves.

I made a list of all the people I knew who had any connection with local media, called them, and got a few interviews in small papers and on radio stations. I sent copies of the book to dream workshops, got it reviewed in a local column on dreams. I sent an announcement of the new edition to old *Comforter* buyers, both individuals and bookstores. The book had sold itself before without reviews. If the Random House promotion system had let me down, I could still count on their distribution system. All they had to do was get it into all the bookstores and it would sell itself again.

They did.

It did. Within a few months the first printing of 10,000 soft-cover copies had sold out. The trouble was that I was the only person who noticed. Phone calls, letters, apologies, assurances, but no action. At the height of the first wave of sales, the book was unavailable, and remained out of print for five months, right into the Christmas season, when half the books published in this country are sold. By the time the second printing of 3,500 was available, it was gone in back orders. The next 3,500 quickly disappeared and another gap followed while, no doubt, Random House waited for returns which did not come. Questions and complaints availed nothing. There seemed to be no clear division of responsibility between my co-publishers and, by this time, little agreement. (After a couple of years Random settled down to printings of 5,000 twice a year, which keep pace with its steady sale.)

I should emphasize that the experiences I'm relating are in no way unusual. Every time I have mentioned these events to another writer, he or she comes up with a horror story which easily tops mine. In late 1977, I was flown to New York to speak at an eight-campus re-entry program where *Ella Price's Journal* was required reading. After my speech, Bob and I went to New York City to visit my new agent. In his office I sat reading through the file of rejection letters he was gathering for my three unpublished novels. The mild objections in these letters were nothing compared to the major change I had been asked to make, and had made, in *Ella*. These were minor, fixable things—the kinds of suggestions made *after* an author has been offered a contract. My old editor at Lippincott was more honest. She liked my fourth novel *Prisoners* and "wanted to publish it," but feared it was not commercial enough. "We probably couldn't sell more than five thousand the first year."

Five thousand used to be considered a good hardback sale to start off with. Now publishers must sell four or five times that many the first year, then quickly sell movie and mass paperback rights, where the real money is. One way to guarantee the six-figure paperback advances we hear about (of which the hard-cover publisher takes half) is to put huge amounts of promotional money behind a few chosen books. A further way to eliminate risk is to manufacture a book, commissioning a writer or writers to do a book on a trendy idea, then orchestrate a book-movie-record ad campaign to assure huge profits before the whole thing drops into oblivion. Some good books slip through this system and get published. Some people win jackpots at Las Vegas, too.

I knew when we came home from that trip that I would go back to self-publishing, but I waited a couple of months before Bob and I sat down to discuss it. This time he was less eager. Not only did he know more about how much work it involved, but he also had other commitments. He had started a plant business in addition to his construction work. And he kept hoping that some day he'd get back to the drawing and painting he'd abandoned in his twenties. He would help, by designing covers and doing the annual tax work and schlepping books to the distributors, but he didn't want to take on any major responsibility. I had to make it clear to him and to myself that I could handle all the petty details of a small business.

Why not? As a teacher I'd corrected thousands of papers, averaged grades, shuffled transcripts. As a writer I'd spent more hours at the typewriter than any office slave, proofreading and rewriting until writing seemed more drudgery than ditch-digging, and less healthful. "Of course, I'll do it," I said, smiling over gritted teeth, "and I'll enjoy it!"

We put the $12,000 I'd taken out of the teachers' retirement system into a business account titled Ata Books. In June 1978 we printed 3,000 of our first title, my six-year-old third novel *Miss Giardino,* a quality paperback priced at $5. Out of that price $1.25 went to the printer and $2.75 to distributors, leaving $1 for promotion and overhead, not to mention my wages as writer, publisher, editor, shipping clerk, bookkeeper. (Production costs have since risen, pushing my price to $6, which I try to hold firm for most of my books.) By November 1978 our first printing was gone, despite sparse reviews. (After sales of 3,000 to 5,000 the first year, *Miss Giardino* settled down to sales of about 1,000 per year. This seems to be the pattern for the books I have published since.)

In 1979 Ata Books published two books: my novel *The Garden of Eros* and my book on the writing process *Writing a Novel,* both in paperback. There were a few more reviews, the most helpful being in *Library Journal,* which gave me the idea that growing library sales might justify publishing in hardcover.

In 1980 Ata Books brought out *Prisoners* simultaneously in hardcover and paperback. It got excellent reviews in national publications which are scanned by librarians and filmmakers. I was interviewed by *Publishers Weekly,* and *Prisoners* was optioned by a major film company. Options rarely turn into movies, but this option (soon dropped) proved that self-published books are not excluded from consideration for those lucrative subsidiary rights.

In 1981 I published my most widely reviewed book, *Killing Wonder.* Labeled a "feminist murder mystery" by some reviewers, it is actually a spoof on "being a writer." Murder mysteries have international appeal; mine is published in England by The Women's Press and was the first of my books to be translated into a foreign language: Danish.

In 1982 Ata Books reissued my first novel, *Ella Price's Journal.* It became the first of my self-published books to be ordered in quantity by one of the chain bookstores and is used in many college classes.

In 1983 I published another novel *A Day In San Francisco*. *Myths To Lie By* brings to eight my present list of self-published books, distributed by wholesalers in the Bay Area, the Midwest, the East Coast, and London.

Ata Books is solvent. My net income is somewhere below the government-designated poverty level, but double the average annual income from writing in the United States. And all my books are in print.

So I have finally found My Publisher.

The next step seems—I'm often told—inevitable. It is, of course, to start publishing other writers. When will I start?

Probably never.

Running my business now takes only five or six hours a week, except during the month I bring out a new book. If I published other writers, I would have to read many manuscripts, then edit, design, produce, and promote books. I would have to revise my primitive but adequate bookkeeping and inventory system to keep track of royalties. Hiring someone else to do all this work would wipe out my small income. Doing it myself would wipe out my writing time.

Besides, dealing with writers would turn me into a nervous wreck. They are such irritating people, with such unrealistic expectations, and such intractable hostility toward publishers!

BOOKS BY DOROTHY BRYANT

Novels

ELLA PRICE'S JOURNAL (paper) $6

THE KIN OF ATA ARE WAITING FOR YOU (paper) $6

MISS GIARDINO (paper) $6

THE GARDEN OF EROS (paper) $6

PRISONERS (paper) $6
(cloth) $10

KILLING WONDER (paper) $6
(cloth) $10

A DAY IN SAN FRANCISCO (paper) $6
(cloth) $12

Non-fiction

WRITING A NOVEL (paper) $5

MYTHS TO LIE BY (paper) $7
(cloth) $13

$1 covers postage for any size order
Californians please add 6% sales tax
Order from

ATA BOOKS
1928 Stuart Street, Berkeley, California 94703